Kerry Birds was born and raised in Derbyshire ...
husband and two young boys. She was introduced to fiction at the
age of thirty-four and took up writing shortly after.

She is both a mother and an Environmental Chemist. Her hobbies include
walking, watching films, and consuming far too many calories.

SHARE MY SKY

Kerry Birds

Acknowledgements

Thank you to my long-suffering husband for tolerating hundreds of nights of me being in 'the zone' and I do apologise, profusely, if I am the sole cause of your turning to beer and social networking.

Thanks to David and Judy. Without your encouragement, I would have abandoned writing long ago.

Thanks to my unpaid proof readers: David (the husband), David, and Shirley. That said, I accept responsibility for any errors which have gone undetected or crept back in.

Chapter 1

Livia

I was hurting.

Really hurting.

Arms. Shoulders. Legs—sitting down and standing up were tortuous. Some women resorted to spanking for their shot of pain but not me, no, I actually paid somebody for a twice weekly bout of discomfort and humiliation during something known as Bootcamp.

Press ups.

Shuttle runs.

Squat thrusts.

Bootcamp: everything which was horrible and nothing which was nice. I sometimes wondered if I was suicidal or sadistic, or if, quite simply, my flings with exhaustion were because expectation was my master—not that I'd have ever admitted it.

Sighing laboriously, I gazed outside.

I lived in a huge Georgian manor house which was converted into luxury apartments—mine having two storeys and floor to ceiling glass paned doors that overlooked the vast, immaculate gardens. The demesne was accessed via wrought-iron gates that would only open following the input of an access code, and the entire garden was surrounded by high sandstone walling and ornate metalwork railings, through which the rolling fields could be seen. My neighbours included a renowned cardiac surgeon, a few barristers, and a retired couple who drove matching Aston Martins—not that I really knew any of them.

I did not care that living in a walled community equated to me partaking in the unofficial apartheid of the British classes. I had worked hard for my situation of privilege. Early mornings. Late nights. Weekends and bank holidays. I had sat in front of a computer through them all.

I sighed again and stroked Edmund, my dog, as the ticking clock announced that another minute of my life had been whittled away. It was seven-thirty and I needed to force my tired body to standing and get ready to go out. And so, the next battle against contentment commenced. Public toilets. Date rape drugs. A murderer driving the hire car. And I was right there, dizzy and nauseous, drugged and violated, generating the cruel scenarios which would lead to my brutal death. I took a deep breath and searched out my multi-coloured capsules of hope: St. John's Wort and Kalms and, just to get me going, a two-hundred milligram dose of caffeine.

I dragged myself to the mirror and fiddled with my fringe until, skimming my lashes, it drifted to the side. My hair was thick, dark, and seemingly unbreakable—regardless of how often I attacked it with the straighteners. Unsurprisingly, after a twelve-hour day, my eyes were slightly puffy, though the lines around them were not yet worth a mention. With a sweep of eyeliner and a bold colour on my lips, I looked confident and poised; inside, however, I was drab and crumbly, with a soul which quivered inside.

After a short rummage in my wardrobe, I selected a pair of black, skinny jeans and a white top which I teamed with a silk scarf. Spiky heels were not going to happen—my tall boots would have to do.

"Hiya, Livia. Glad you made my send off!"

Ellen, my valued colleague, got to her feet. I gave her a hug.

"Wouldn't miss it for the world." I pulled the small wrapped envelope from my handbag and handed it to her. "This is from me and Edmund. Well, Edmund really—you know what he's like when he gets his furry paws on my credit card," I blathered.

Ellen fiddled with the ribbon and opened the envelope.

"Oh, Liv. Theatre tickets. Thankyou. Thank you so much."

And for those, I got another hug. Ellen was still beaming, rattling off the shows they would like to see, when the others arrived, drinks in hand.

I flitted my eyes around the wine bar as I pursed my lips around my straw. We had settled in the corner where the lights were honeyed and soft, and the raised beech floor gave an excellent view of the room. The bar area, all lovely with its cream wooden cladding and slate surfaces, was littered with people. Some, straight from the office, wore tailoring which would never fall out of fashion, though many were in high-street garments which would look dated before the season was out. Bold colours. Garish patterns. Sleeves stretched too tight across muscles and skirts which revealed too much leg. Some people laughed politely, amused though reserved, though others cackled like witches, all deportment cast aside. To these revellers I cast my shameful disapproval and to my shameful disapproval I attributed shame; I did not want to feel prejudice but, to a certain extent, life makes judges of us all.

My view landed on a small gathering of young men sitting near to the window and I tried very hard not to gape at the dark-haired man in my line of sight. There were no two ways about it, if he earned another sixty-grand a year I would offer to buy him a drink—but with those clothes and that poise he wasn't wealthy enough to keep up with me: posh restaurants, exotic holidays and retail therapy were the key to my happiness. Happiness? I chose not to dwell. I sucked a little harder and heard the skittering of the last drops of liquid as they lost contact with the ice in my glass.

"I'll go for another round of drinks!"

I grabbed my bag from the table and headed to the bustling bar, the noise thickening as I approached. At the far end, there was a small group consisting of two women and four men, all suited and booted, trying to avoid the rowdy gathering of male students besides them. The students wore green Rugby tops and had pints of lager and whiskey chasers lined up before them. To their right was a space and then the blonde guy who accompanied the dark-haired sex god.

"What can I get you?" the bartender asked him.

He flipped a big palm in my direction. "Serve this lady first."

"No, it was you," I twittered.

"Please, serve her fir…"

Before there was the time to finish the word, I was knocked, hard, in the middle of the back. Taking one, two, and then three steps forward, I fell into the bar and dropped my purse. Stunned and shaking, I went to collect the cards which littered the floor though the blonde guy beat me to it. He gathered the coloured plastic into a disorderly pile and dumped it, along with a damp twenty-pound note, into the cup of my outstretched palms.

"Thank you."

The guy gave me a little smile. He was intense, painfully intense, and I was transfixed.

He stepped around me and tapped a burly guy between the shoulders. "What do you say to the lady you knocked over?"

"It. Was. An. Accident," my assailant spat, his lip curled.

"I couldn't give a rat's ass whether it was accidental or you have the second-by-second countersigned plot in your pocket. You nearly put her face into the bar. What do you say?"

As the suited group turned sheepishly away from the aggravation, the stare belonging to the arrogant student was joined by that belonging to one of his friends. The blonde guy pointed at him.

"And you can wipe that look off your face an'all. You ought to be ashamed of yourself using the language I just heard in front of a woman."

The foul-mouthed student curled his fingers around a pint glass and said 'come on, lads' to his friends.

"Oy. You," barked my knight in not so shining armour.

He took two steps closer to my assailant and said something into his ear; my assailant, appearing suitably shamefaced, looked at me and said 'sorry'. I nodded and turned back to the bar.

"Thank you," I said again.

The blonde guy gave me another reserved smile and looked firmly forward. I gave my order to the barman who then diligently scurried away. I tried, I really did, but my damn roving eyes kept veering to the stranger. His hair needed a cut, he looked like he had not seen a razor in days, and the collar tips of his blue shirt curled slightly—my suspicion being due to poor quality rather than a lack of ironing. His hands were flat on the bar; the fingernails were short and square and the knuckles slightly roughened. I wondered what his skin felt like; I wondered how my hand would fit into his; I wondered if the grip on my sanity was finally lost.

A tall glass appeared before me, the ice cubes fighting for space and the orange-red liquid fading to yellow, and I caught a glimpse of my reflection in the mirrored wall behind the optics. Bugger. He had seen my not-so-subtle observations though he was ignoring me and I was strangely devastated.

Another bar attendant took his order as the last of my drinks landed. My server snatched a straw from a black, plastic tube and attempted to throw it, dart-like, into my tequila sunrise. It missed and, to my horror, he picked it up and put it into my glass. I handed over my credit card and felt the blush on my face match that of the rising Grenadine in my drink.

My head swirled.

I looked into my glass and considered how many hands had touched the surface where the straw landed; and those hands, they could have come into contact with anything—dirty toilets, raw chicken, animal excrement—the possibilities were endless. I estimated the alcohol content of the drink and decided it insufficient to kill any bacteria which might be present. I could not drink that cocktail and so summoned the barman to prepare another.

"Excuse me, 'ow much are the ready salted crisps, please?" the blonde guy asked.

"Eighty-five pence," the barman replied, tugging a packet of crisps from an overhead cardboard strip.

I keyed in my PIN as the alluring man emptied the contents of his tatty wallet onto the bar. He put two pounds and eighteen pence into a pile, counted out the remaining coppers and then huffed.

"Cheers mate, but you better put them back."

The bartender nodded at the other pile of coins. "What about that?"

"Bus money."

My stomach plunged as I rifled in my bag for a pound coin. "Put a packet on my next bill."

He looked at me, smiling as he shook his head. "No, but thanks all the same."

I checked out his eyes; they were bright and deep—the dark blue broken by white lightening in a stormy sky. I was feeling poetic and romanticised and totally out of sorts. Perhaps I'd been drugged—I was a sensible, objective person and nobody had stirred anything other than pragmatism in me for as long as I could remember.

He split the jumble of unallocated coins between the RSPCA and Barnardo's collection boxes on the bar, grabbed his beer, and left me stranded. Stranded and humbled. He had stood up to somebody on behalf of a total stranger and then gave his last seventy-four pence to charity—I didn't realise people like him still existed. I had monthly direct debits for a few charities and bought the odd herd of goats for the poor in Africa, but my giving was no sacrifice—in all honesty, I could have donated a thousand pounds a month and not noticed. Unlike him.

I arranged my glasses on a tray, leaving the contaminated one behind, and returned to the table where I downed my cocktail before hurrying back to the bar for more drinks and a packet of ready salted crisps. Fuelled by Dutch courage, I inhaled deeply and strode over to his table. The blonde guy raised his brows in question.

"You left your crisps on the bar."

I dared not to breathe as the confusion crossed his features. I hoped, so hoped, he was not about to shoot me down. I swallowed hard.

"Thank you."

He took the packet and his fingers touched mine. I wanted to ask his name; I wanted to know what music he liked; I wanted to find out where he came from and where he wanted to go. But instead I said nothing at all and scurried away.

I was shell-shocked.

I needed to get drunk.

Chapter 2

Russ

People are complex things.

All different.

Acting or responding.

Disregarding or interacting.

And very rarely, they shake another by the thoughts until that person can't remember what they were doing, where they have been, or what the hell they are meant to do next.

It had never happened to me before. Not until I met the eyes of the woman who emptied her purse on the floor. She felt important to me and I wasn't sure why. I didn't know if she was tall or short; I didn't know if she was voluptuous or thin; I didn't know if she was wearing a cocktail dress or a pair of tatty Primark leggings. All I knew was that I ought to drink up and leave before I saw her again. But, as it turned out, I'd become Captain Stupid and I wasn't going anywhere.

I took a mouthful of the thick, dark ale and cleared my top lip of the froth. My brother, Zac, took another drink and smiled with his eyes. I returned a grin. We didn't need words. Zac was my only sibling and my polar opposite. He was light-hearted and didn't over think things like me. He was outgoing and friendly, what with his tales and goofy smiles, whereas I shied away from most people. I'd probably been with slightly fewer women than average, but him, god, I hated to think. When faced with a woman Zac traded his brain for a cock like a hammer action drill—wives, girlfriends, his best mate's mother—he'd even shagged a nun. I'd never said it out loud but I loved my bro. And he loved me. One time I broke my legs jumping off a pier to save him from drowning; one time he had his legs broken because he lied to a drug lord and said he was the brother who told his scummy underling to stop bothering the kids on the park. Yeah, we were tight—we always had been.

I laughed after his latest round of yammer and then searched the room for the beautiful woman from the bar. I finally saw her in the far corner. She was wearing a white blouse which glowed under the lights and one of those posh scarf things bunched up around her neck. Her legs were crossed, a booted foot bouncing nervously, and she twiddled her glass in her hands. God, she was hot. Dark, shoulder-length hair. Amber eyes. The sort of lips a fella's dreams are made of.

I wanted to talk to her, I really did, but a massive social boundary was between us—all covered in razor wire and glossy posters showing political lies and social untruths. She was taught, proud, and predictable: her bag contained the latest iPhone, a lipstick which cost thirty pounds, and enough plastic to build a raft. I was nonchalant and hairy and I looked about as predictable as a pick-and-mix sack of venomous snakes. She was Homo Sapiens; I was closer to Neanderthal man; some things were not meant to be.

Trying not to look like a weird stalker, I glanced around the room. I met her eye and took my drink in hand. A corner of her mouth lifted as she looked away, all coy like. I took a big gulp. The woman made a hole in my side and got right under my skin—in spite of being one of the stuck-up, privileged rich who went against everything I believed in. Still, I was taken by her wrinkled nose and the disapproving scowl she shot at the non-rich kids nearby. And I couldn't look away when she pulled out a pair of sexy-as-fuck glasses and perched them on her nose. My grin was still there when I filled my mouth with beer. I had no idea why she was giving me the eye— she could have her pick of anybody in the bar.

I got to my feet and saw her wobble to standing. Yeah, she was pissed— that explained a lot. I looked at her, her stare firmly on me, and remembered the expression on my brother's face when she came to the table; he was taking up arms for the charm offensive and imagining what he wanted to do with her.

I suddenly felt it in my head. In my guts. In every fibre of my being.

Between them, Zac and the woman had ripped open an old wound and I was bleeding, really bleeding, and struggling to rein it all in. And right then, right that second, I knew if he ever touched her I would kill him. There were no two ways about it. I'd kill my own flesh and blood.

She was walking in my direction, her lithe hips swinging, trying to persuade me to abandon logic and turn feral. I wondered what it would be like to kiss those lips. Just once. I couldn't see her condescending attitude or her John Lewis store card though I saw the question—the what if—in her eyes.

"T, what the hell are you thinking?" Zac chirped. "You look like your mind's on the moon."

"I'm goin' home," I returned.

And my feet couldn't get me out of there quick enough.

I'd not made it far down the street when I heard the tap, tap, tapping sound of women's shoes. I knew it was her without looking.

"Excuse me."

I turned around to see her doing one of those knees together, ankles kicking, high heeled runs.

"Everything alright?" I stopped in my tracks.

The woman smiled shyly and nodded. The white from the street lights made her look enchanting—like a goddess or a white witch.

"Thanks for sticking up for me," she finally said, her words tense and shaky.

I did a half-arsed shrug. "Should have never come to that—bloody students—if they can't take their beer…"

She smiled at me and my stomach turned into a moulded jelly wobbling on a plate. I looked at her, saying nothing, and she looked right back at me, her eyes twinkling and as wide as a full moon. And I was there—we were there—in one of those films where two people are standing in a silent street and blurry, faceless people are whooshing past. I looked at her boots; the toes were close and she clicked the heels together as she fidgeted with her feet. I shifted my weight from foot to foot. I didn't know what to say and, judging by her lack of words, neither did she. I wondered why she'd given chase.

"I, erm…" Her eyebrows scrunched together, like she was totally confused. "I erm…"

A white bus swung around the corner and stopped with a noisy hiss of the brakes. The number eighty-two: my chariot.

"I've gotta go," I told her.

The woman nodded and bit her lip and I marched off, leaving a trail of marbles in my wake.

As usual, the bus smelled of upholstery cleaner and B.O. and I took a seat in the middle, away from the over-excited teenagers at the back. I glanced out of the window. She was still there, her arms hanging by her sides, looking fucked up and forlorn like a kid dumped at a children's home. She held up her hand, to say goodbye, and I did the same.

I wanted to get off the bus and ask her what she wanted to say; I wanted to tell her I thought she was beautiful and I sensed some really weird shit going down between us. But I couldn't stick around and talk with her. I didn't want to feel the happiness before it all came crashing down. And it would because, with the hand I'd been dealt, I'd never be lucky enough to have her. Rationality kept my fingers away from the red button which would stop the bus and good sense glued me to the chair.

I had a family to think about and a life to rebuild.

I'd hit rock bottom already and I couldn't face the thought of going there again.

Chapter 3

Livia

I closed the lid on my Mac and muttered a few unimportant words to my dog as two figures crossed my line of sight. I immediately recognised one as Alan, the aged, stooped gardener who had recently told me he was retiring at the grand-old age of sixty-seven, but the other man was unknown to me. He sauntered half a step behind Alan with his hands in his utility trouser pockets and his dark-blonde-haired head nodding periodically. Yes, I was nosey and, as such, I told Edmund to fetch his lead and bounced from the settee. I had put on my Hunter wellies and made it to the door before him.

As I strode towards the unlikely pair, I ran a few fingers through my hair and wished I'd powdered my nose and applied some lip gloss rather than falling out of the door like my house was burning around me. Alan turned around after hearing the panting of either my dog or me—I couldn't be sure.

"Afternoon, Livia."

"Hiya, Alan."

The other man turned too.

Oh my gosh.

It was him: Alan's accomplice was the blonde guy who ran away from me after the wine bar and the image of him I kept in my head was in no way enhanced by intoxication. The man towered above Alan's hunched frame—his unruly hair adding a good inch to his height. Up close and in the bright natural light, I could see he was a little younger than me and well-built without the bulking. He met my eyes, grinning shyly; I smiled back and tucked some hair behind my ear. I looked up from my mud-smeared wellies to find him rubbing the short beard on his cheek, gnawing his lip.

"Russell, this lovely young lady is Livia—she lives in number two. Livia, this is Russell. He's the new me—gardener, groundskeeper, forester—jack of all trades and master of none," Alan said, cheerily.

"Nice to meet you, Livia. I'm Russ. And who's this?"

Russ offered the back of his hand to my dog.

I was both relieved and impressed. Edmund was a skittish character. I hated meeting people who dived straight in, reaching for his face and ears with their fingers outstretched, because they made him nervous and nervous made him snappy. But there was none of that. Edmund had a little sniff of his hand and then met it with the side of his nose.

"He's, erm, Edmund," I told him.

Russ scratched Edmund behind the collar. "I can't make you out, Ed—are you a Greyhound with obesity?"

"He's, erm, a Weimaraner."

"He's mint—aren't ya lad!" Russ returned, on his haunches, stroking behind Edmund's ears.

Edmund was taken. Totally taken. Tail wagging, gazing at Russ like he was the next best thing to a bouncy ball, taken. And I was taken too, to be fair. Neither Kieran, my current male interest, nor any of my previous companions had ever gravitated to my dog. He was the inconvenience I needed to be home for after a day out; the reason I couldn't take a weekend away at short notice; the mutt who put the occasional silver hair on their dark trousers. He was the dog who, after a bit of rough play, jumped at Russ and put him flat on his back on the muddy grass.

Shit. Shit.

I grabbed Edmund's collar and pulled him away.

"Oh my gosh. I am so sorry. You're a bad dog," I snapped at Edmund, jabbing my finger. "I'm so sorry. I don't know what came over him. He's not usually…. he's…"

Russ got to his feet and brushed the grass from his ass. "Don't worry. Really," he said, grinning. "I like dogs. Always wanted one."

"Why don't you get one?"

Russ kicked his toes into the dirt and shrugged. "Food. Vet's bills. Ya know. Anyway, I've never been at home enough to look after a dog. One day!" He smiled, shy and reluctant, and stroked Edmund's head.

My eyes wandered past Russ' face. Unlike Alan and I, who were wrapped up in coats, Russ only wore a long-sleeved t-shirt, the sleeves hitched to the elbow, on which the seam had come undone on the collar. My view lingered a little too long on his neck—soft skin, broken with the odd whisker, his Adam's apple shifting as he swallowed.

"Livia," Alan said; "are you alright?"

"Oh, gosh, yes. Must have zoned out! Not enough sleep last night," I quipped.

My behaviour was very atypical. I usually rattled away, laughed and joked: I did not look at the floor, coy and nervous, and I did not stare at men.

Following our somewhat strange introduction, I chirped away and asked Russ many questions. Where did he work now? When would he start at the manor? Did he think the cold weather would bother him? On and on I went, rabbiting like a nervous girl as I twisted the dog lead around my fingers. Russ handled my interrogation with polite but to the point answers though he hardly looked at me at all. Realising that I was coming across as a total fruitcake, I turned my attention to Alan who, as always, was happy to chat. The new guy seemed happy to listen but I needed to get on. I did not want to appear needy and the dog walk was unscheduled. I had a dinner-dance that evening and my 'date' was due to collect me at seven. I told Alan to drop by before he left, said it was nice to meet Russ, and got on my way.

I waited at the door in my towering heels, black dress, and with a perfectly made-up face. *What am I like?* I asked myself rhetorically. After meeting with Russ, I was snatched from my day of indifference and slung into a cataclysm in which several fantasies (involving the lady of the manor and her rugged gardener) jostled for my attention. I wanted to see what was under those well-worn clothes; I wanted to know if the soft hair on his top lip and chin would tickle when he kissed me; I wanted to know how he would feel between my legs.

I glanced at my watch and, disappointedly, it was one minute to seven and Kieran would be here any time. The thoughts bouncing around my head were so naughty I seriously debated whether I could get myself off in the downstairs loo before the car arrived and if it would be obvious on my face. I suspected the answer to the first question was yes—I was really on one, thinking about Russ. The answer to the second question was also yes but I didn't care. I was awaiting collection by an escort for heaven's sake: a man I paid to stand by my side and offer educated comments for an evening. Oh and, on occasion, the services offered by that particular man extended beyond the employment brief. Not that I ever paid him for sex; I didn't oppose it but he was offended the first time I offered money and so I left it there. I got the impression he would happily go out with me for free but it was not an option. Kieran and I were a business transaction because that was how I wanted it. I got the companionship I needed from my furry, faithful friend: the one who was grey with floppy ears; he was a bit stupid and could be highly strung on occasion but he was a Weimaraner and I knew the score when I got him. Not that I hadn't had boyfriends—they came and went as they took the energy and time I wanted to funnel into my job. The escorting worked well; I often needed male company for business events and after landing upon Kieran things worked very well.

Kieran was hot. And when I say hot, I don't just mean the kind of man you walk past in the street and think 'yeah I would': he was the sort of man who made your mouth drop open before you started inwardly dropping expletives. He was dark-haired, blue-eyed, tall and broad, and was obscenely alluring in a tuxedo. He was smarter than your average Joe; he had a Master's in Business Management, owned his own company, earned at least a hundred grand a year, and he shared my sentiments where relationships were concerned. He flattered my ego, I flattered his, and he was professional enough to accept payment to ensure we were absolutely not in a relationship.

Hmmm. I would not be getting myself off in the loo. A large black car pulled up outside and six and a half feet of man exited it with a smile. He arrived at the door at the same time as me and the dog: the dog who, incidentally, offered my visitor a look of distain and skulked off to his bed.

"Livia, looking as stunning as ever," Kieran growled, as he kissed me on one cheek and then the other.

"Likewise." I locked up and linked his arm as we walked to the car. "Have you had a good day?"

He shot me one of his million-dollar smiles, closed the car door, and then entered the vehicle on the other side. "Yes. I took Esme to the farm park and then we had dinner at some godforsaken burger shop on the way home."

Esme was his six-year-old daughter and she was another reason Kieran hadn't had a serious relationship since he split with his ex-wife, Kimberly.

He did not want to share his weekends with anybody else and women invariably got grumpy due to the amicable relationship he shared with his ex.

"Did you bring me the toy from the Happy Meal?" I teased.

"No, but I'll show you my toy later."

I shook my head and playfully slapped his thigh. "Kieran, I'm paying you from seven to eleven 'o' clock and I expect my employees to behave during working hours."

"I hope you don't expect me to behave after. I've not seen you for weeks and my thoughts have been particularly impure since I got home," he said, flatly.

There was that to mention too. Oh, yes, the story only deepened. Kieran and I were exclusive and we had been for almost a year; it was neither discussed nor agreed, it just happened and, in all honesty, our relationship was fucked up. Once a month we met for coffee and studied our diaries. I told him when I wanted him and he told me when he was available—not because of other women but because his job took him abroad and he had pre-arranged dates when he saw his little girl. We usually met two or three times a month, generally to attend my business engagements but occasionally just to go on a 'date'—we socialised, ate and drank, and often had sexual relations. In-between there were no friendly phone calls, text messages, or chats via social networking, and we only made contact on a need-to-know basis. It was the best of both worlds and it suited us fine.

As usual, the company between us was easy and fluent. We discussed things which had occurred since our last meeting and laughed and joked. That was another good thing about our relationship—we'd always got something to talk about and, more importantly, we never talked about paying the bills, arranging the travel insurance for the next holiday, putting out the recycling, or emptying the dishwasher. Forty-minutes later we arrived and I slid along the soft, cream leather and exited the car.

The hors d'oeuvres appeared on silver trays, borne by men and women wearing white cotton gloves and starched uniforms. I loved the tiny little satellites of colour: small circles of soft cheese surrounded by smoked salmon or chorizo, and tiny squares of Melba toast adorned with fresh crab pate or slithers of pink beef and Horseradish. I always wanted them but I never would. I couldn't do finger food and only ever ate the things which circulated with cocktail sticks to stab the morsel—a stuffed olive or a juicy, pink prawn maybe.

The men in suits joked and exchanged trivia and I laughed politely and answered the questions which I was asked. I didn't command without prompt—I left Kieran to do that. I used my intelligence to indulge their inflated egos because it served me best. My job was to be the interesting observer, that was until it came to finance, investment, and fund management, and then with reserve and confidence I knocked off their socks. I was an expert: a seasoned professional who could dance the dance, play the game, and get the results when it mattered.

Kieran grabbed my attention prior to being seated.

"Are you sure we're okay going back to yours tonight, Livia?"

I smiled. "Yes. Why wouldn't we be?"

"You seem somewhat distracted. Are you well?"

"Yes, I'm fine." *I just can't help thinking about the new gardener.* "I need to visit the washroom. See you at the table."

My stud of a date took hold of my forearm and kissed my cheek. I smiled and headed to the ladies', my mind lost among the fairies.

I hated public toilets—even those which were shiny and opulent. I could not stand the thought of sitting on a toilet seat which had been previously used by a stranger, and the thought of their bodily functions made my stomach turn. I could not even enter a bathroom which smelled of another person's poo because odour was caused by molecules which meant tiny bits of faecal matter were entering my nose, my lungs....

I felt the anxiety rise, thought back to my failed attempts at cognitive behavioural therapy, CBT, and started to go through the mental motions. I went into the cubicle, closed the door, and used a piece of toilet tissue from the dispenser to secure the lock. The arm of the lock was chrome and polished until reflective but it still looked sinister. I did not sit on the toilet seat but instead hovered above it. I flushed the toilet with a piece of folded toilet paper and then used it to open the door before throwing it into the pan. To my relief, the soap and taps were sensor triggered and I squirted six shots of soap into my hands before washing them thoroughly. From my bag, I produced a small tube of moisturising cream and rubbed some of it into my hands before leaving the ladies'.

Kieran, as polite as ever, got to his feet when I reached the table. He pulled out my chair and kissed my hand. He was a great actor though he wasn't half as good as me.

The particular gathering of people with which I was sharing/wasting an evening of my life were a predictable bunch.

James. Grey lustrous trousers, no tie, white fitted shirt, the top few buttons open—not bad looking—overly confident. At a guess, he was in sales before sidestepping and, by good luck rather than judgement, climbing the ladder to his current position in banking.

Keely. James' fiancé, sitting by his side—eyes wide and guileless—afraid of talking for fear of embarrassing James in front of the 'important people'—seduced by his ego and not his substandard sexual performance.

Lucy. Mousy hair trying to escape a sensible twist—shoulders pushed back and hands folded in her lap, deliberate and unnatural—probably her second or third dinner event—her eyes rheumy because she'd thought it necessary to exchange the glasses for contact lenses—exceptionally intelligent though more suited to academia—she'd be on Prozac before her thirtieth birthday.

Neil. Late forties, his hair spiked in an attempt to make him look younger—sitting back in his chair, a hand flopped on the table—astute, competent, experienced—he would retire at fifty-five and his marriage would fail soon after because, due to his long working hours and subsequent absence from home, his wife had built a new life and he had no place in it.

On and on, around the table. Ten others, in addition to us. Dry-clean only clothes. Considered body language. Carefully chosen words. People in periods of professional growth, others at the pinnacle of professional excellence. Everybody acting up to Kieran and I because I was the most influential person present and he was with me. And we looked perfect together.

"So, Livia," Neil piped up; "we were discussing investment in countries with expanding economies. What's your view on Nigeria?"

I twisted my wine glass by the stem and took a tiny sip. "Not right now. Financial management is not simply about economies: it's about politics too. And politically, I'm uncertain about many countries—Nigeria being one of them."

The gentleman before me raised a heavy brow. "And do you follow world politics?"

"Yes. My first degree was in politics and financial economics. It was only during my MSc that I focused on financial risk management," I added, flippantly.

Kieran grinned smugly. "So, politics and finance. What does that make you?"

"Boring!" I exclaimed, instigating a round of polite laughs.

"No, Livia, that makes you useful," Kieran returned. "Very useful."

I offered him a smile though I suddenly felt hollow. *Useful.* I was an asset. Kieran saw me as an asset: a catalyst to link him with contacts to benefit his business: the person who managed his affairs and inflated his bank account. And those around saw me as an asset too—that was why they vouched for my arguments and laughed at my remarks. Though, I supposed, asset management was an inevitable part of life—for those who did well in it anyway.

The meal, all faultlessly cooked and neatly presented, was delightful but uninspiring; the post-meal speech, both informative and perfectly dispersed with one-liners, was well constructed but unexciting; the after-speech conversation, while fluent and well-humoured, was uneventful and bland.

All in all, another night of my sterile life had been consumed though I still, and with uttermost conviction, told the chairman of the board that I'd had a 'lovely night'. I didn't tell him that the social ritual had become like the faking of an orgasm with the hope that going through the motions would make it happen. And I had faked the happiness but it had not happened and I still felt empty and devoid.

Yes. Devoid was most definitely how I felt.

And I couldn't wait to leave.

The car ride home was a word-filled affair. Kieran and I discussed the latest politically motivated internet beheading and laughed about the latest useless bit of plastic out of the Happy Meal. He sat at one side of the cream leather seat and I on the other. We did not touch or hold hands though the verbal foreplay began; it was certain we would be sexually intimate within the next hour.

We arrived back at my house, I changed my shoes, put on some gloves, and took Edmund for a walk as Kieran made us coffee. The walk was short and I was back in the fold within ten-minutes. I removed my wellies at the door and the dog waited on the mat while I got the designated cloth and towel to clean his feet. There were two mugs of coffee on the kitchen counter but before collecting one I looked at the three chrome and glass containers in the corner. I switched their positions, like a magician hiding a coin under a cup, and returned them to the correct places.

Coffee. Sugar. Tea. Alphabetical order. If they were left in the wrong order I could run out without noticing or something even worse could happen—like Edmund getting ill or me losing a big client.

After drinking the coffee, Kieran led me to the bedroom. As soon as we crossed the threshold we were kissing, our clothes hitting my deep-pile carpet. I lay on the bed and his face went south; my breaths hitched in anticipation. I liked oral sex and I liked kissing but we couldn't do both. I would have to roll over after and encourage him to take me from behind. Still, his mouth was very persuasive and I reached orgasm quickly and then bent over the bed. I heard the rip of a packet and soon after he was inside me. Later, I touched myself to join him in his orgasm and collapsed on the sheets as the judges displayed their cards.

Technique: 6, 6, and 5.8.

Effort: 5.8, 5.9, and 6.

Enjoyment: the judges declined to comment.

Chapter 4

Livia

Edmund paced back and forth like a wild animal caged. He was usually pacified with a fresh bowl of water and a dental chew when I arrived home but he was having none of it. I'd got up at five-am to take him out before I left for the office at six-thirty; I was delivering a presentation at nine and so wanted to be there in advance to prepare. He, like me, was not a natural early riser and was as enthusiastic as a cat at the vet's during his morning walk. My cleaner was due that morning and I paid her extra to take him out for a good run when she finished at two. It was four-thirty and, judging by his levels of hyperactivity, he'd either spent the entire day munching blue Smarties or she had not quite done as she promised. When the pacing extended to a walk, a spin-turn, and then a snot shower on the window, I gave in.

Due to the impulsive nature of my outing, I decided to stay in my grey woollen dress and add wellies and a coat to complete the uncoordinated look. Oh, and a pair of gloves. It wasn't cold but I always wore gloves if I could get away with it, clean ones of course, because the thought of bacteria and scratches could make me anxious to the point of mental exhaustion. I knew it was ridiculous but, some days, I could wash my hands ten times and they still felt dirty.

Edmund retrieved his lead from the hall and we were off to meet the drizzly wind and fresh air. I kept him on the leash along the periphery wall, past the formal rose garden, and to the once prim area that the new gardener seemed to be leaving to run amok at the very bottom of the grounds. Here I reached the fenced-off dog area and Edmund's skinny legs were running before I unclipped his lead. I liked to watch the crazy little mutt and his canine enthusiasm; he always took the same route, crossing the area, nose down like a retriever, searching out the rabbits, badgers, and foxes I assumed. Once the tracking was completed it was time for him to fetch the stick until my arm ached, and then he emptied his bladder and it was time to go.

We took the longer route back which followed the wall anticlockwise and led past the stone-built groundskeeper's hut. My heart quickened as we approached. I hadn't really seen much of Russ since he started and we only exchanged a polite hello when our paths crossed. He kept to himself but, aside of the wild patch, he was doing an exceptional job in the gardens—even taking on the unrulier bushes and tall trees which I suspected Alan shied away from as he aged. As we got closer I saw that the hut was illuminated and the old, silvery door slightly ajar. Oh, and low and behold, my bloody dog, which had got it right on him, pulled his lead out of my gloved hand and bolted towards the hut.

Arse.

"Edmund. Come back here."

Yes, I ought to have saved my breath. Three-seconds later, I tapped on the door and gingerly peered at the man who was on his haunches, scratching my dog's head in a way that I thought looked painful. Edmund, his tongue out and his head thrown back, obviously loved a bit of rough.

"Hi, erm, sorry, he erm," I stammered.

He was the chalk to the cheese of every man I'd dated since high school but I still fancied him like mad. Not that it would ever be an option because, well, he just wasn't like me. We were from different worlds. Without a shared past or the subject of business we would have nothing to talk about; given the way he manhandled my dog, we would be incompatible in bed; and considering what I saw at the bar, we could not even find shared ground over wine, cars, and foreign holidays.

No.

We would never work.

The gardener looked up and smiled a broad smile; I assumed it was a very broad smile but it was hard to tell—he seemingly hadn't shaved for a good week.

"He's alright. I don't mind him barging in."

Russ looked at me intently. Good gosh—those eyes—they really were an electrical storm. Stunning. Intense. But so warm and kind. Shrinking under his stare, I slapped my thigh.

"Edmund, come here. Sorry to bother you, Russ."

Edmund clearly wanted to stay and wandered off to the corner, sat in front of the small convection heater, and sniffed hopefully in the direction of a packet of biscuits on the worktop beside the square ceramic sink.

Russ looked at the dog and grinned. "Looks like he wants to stay for a biscuit. Stop for a cup of tea if ya like."

I glanced at the kettle beside the biscuits and I felt it straight away. It started like a stone in my stomach that sent out tendrils into my limbs, making them feel as though they were quaking even though they were perfectly still. I really wanted to stay for ten-minutes with the young man and so started to make my light-speed justifications.

The water will be boiling. Don't take milk.

"Erm, yes, that would be lovely, thank you. Would you like me to make it?"

He eyed me suspiciously—it was mightily odd for a stranger to offer to make her own drink.

"Err. Knock yourself out," he said. "I have milk an' one sugar."

"Okay," I chirped, feeling like the mentalist who I knew I looked.

Beside the kettle, there was a large plastic tub which contained the cups. There were three mismatched mugs—one red, one with a faded PG tips monkey on the front, and one white and chipped. To my relief, they all looked clean and the teabags were in the box and were definitely dry.

I filled the kettle, added the tea bags to the cups, put the teaspoon in one of them, and left it a good while after the boiling water was added. I tended to the drinks as he titivated around, putting tools in their haphazard homes and arranging things on the surfaces. It all looked a jumble to me but the whole place was strangely calm.

He produced a deckchair and erected it a little way from the reclaimed armchair which was there already. Russ indicated for me to take the comfy chair and got the biscuits from the side. I pulled down my coat and perched on the soft chair as I nursed my drink. He stuck his fingertip in the side of the biscuit packet and urged one to pop out of the top. The first digestive went to my panting, salivating dog and then he offered the packet to me. I hesitated before pulling out a biscuit on which I nibbled. The bit between my thumb and first finger went to the dog. And then we proceeded to eat the biscuits with the sparsest exchange of words I could recall in my adult life. But there was no discomfort and, for the first time in as long as I could remember, there was no pressure to perform—sell my attributes, convince people of my goodness, provide interest, or make people laugh. It was novel and, above all, precious. With his stillness and patience, he was yoga, a spa weekend, and an aromatherapy massage all rolled into one.

"Nice tea—you make a decent cuppa, Livia. I like your dog an' all."

I smiled back at him but shied from the eye contact. "Nice hut."

"Yeah, I like it."

I was overwhelmed by his lack of sell and I was totally sold. I was used to meeting men who held out their hands and came forward with a, 'hello, I do this. I want that. I am going there and I can give you this'. It was a big reason I took Kieran everywhere; without bragging, I was quite a catch—pretty enough, slim, and very successful, and bachelors gravitated to me with their annoying claims of suitability. All Russ did was throw a biscuit to my dog, wiggle another one free for himself, and pass me the packet. I reached inside to find it empty.

Russ paused with the biscuit in mid-air before closing his mouth and offering it to me. "Sorry. I never realised it was the last one."

I instinctively reached out to accept his offer of kindness and then stopped. His large hands were marred with the efforts of his day and the tips of his thumb and fingers were definitely not clean. My eyes revealed my anxiety and I swallowed audibly.

"Please have it, Livia. I can't eat the last biscuit—I've bin brought up better than that."

"No, you have it. I can't erm—" *Eat something that has been in a dirty hand.*

"Are you immune suppressed or summot?"

I shook my head and looked back at the biscuit. It was only a digestive biscuit, plain packaging, home-brand, but I really did want it. I was starving. I'd worked through lunch and dinner seemed an age away.

"Well, a bit of muck won't kill you."

He had noticed my observations and interpreted my actions. Neither my friends, family, Kieran nor work colleagues had ever made the link in countless hours of shared company. The only person to whom I had even mentioned it was my therapist, and that was under duress.

"I haven't got time for setbacks like illness and the biscuit might make me ill," I fretfully said— admitting a negative thought pattern to someone I hardly knew.

"Chances are, it won't make you ill."

And I felt it: I felt those nasty tendrils of anxiety curling their way into my limbs, tightening my stomach and shooting adrenaline into my blood.

"Anyway," he continued, "we've all got a shelf life—we ain't got time to avoid doing stuff we want and regret not doin' it. Chance means it doesn't always go tits up so we won't need to regret every time. So, if we do sumthin', and only have to regret what we do sometimes, then we must be saving time in the long run."

I laughed and the tendrils retracted.

"Russ, I have absolutely no idea what you just said."

"Nah, neither do I." Russ started to laugh too and then he stopped, looking thoughtful. "My dad sez two steps forward and one step back is the makin' of a person. Reckons somebody never appreciates the good if they never av it bad. Risk the setback. It might be worth it."

I nodded—the gesture seemed enough with him.

He offered the biscuit again and I could not believe the thought-provoking, life-changing shit which was going on over a single sodding biscuit.

"Do you want it?"

I nodded again. "I suppose I do."

"Right, stop worrying about things that might never happen and eat it."

I took the biscuit from his grubby hand and ate the lot. All of those months of talking about bad thought identification and breaking negative behavioural patterns and I was dealing with things head on.

With him.

Exposure therapy: the thing I staunchly refused.

I took an item of food from a man who had been touching soil and who might not wash his hands after visiting the toilet, and I put it in my mouth. I ate the biscuit. I ate the biscuit because Russ, in that haphazard scruffy sanctuary, didn't offer me sympathy, mumbo-jumbo, or a list of justifications: he gave me the simple honest voice of reason.

No bullshit.

No elaborate words.

He held out his hand and, unknowingly, offered to walk me through something of which I was afraid. And for some reason, I wanted to take his hand when I had secretly refused that of others.

Russ and me chatted a little more before I noticed the time and said I really did have to go. I didn't want to. I wanted to stay with him and for the life of me I could not pinpoint why.

"Would you mind if I came again?" My words were impulsive and I regretted them immediately.

"I have absolutely no idea why I like you, Livia," Russ said, sounding puzzled.

My face went red as I looked at my wellies.

"No, neither do I," I admitted. At no point had I tried to prove my worth to him and I couldn't see what he could like. Quite frankly, I had done nothing but exhibit my weirdness. "And I have no idea why I like you with bluntness like that."

Russ pointed to a very clean spade that was propped against the wall.

"What's that, Livia?"

"A spade."

He nodded. "Aye. I call a spade a spade. If you go around telling people a spade is a fork, you can't complain when some dumb-ass takes the spade and tries to use it like one."

"No, I don't suppose you can."

"Come back if you like—just don't expect me to call a spade anything other than a spade. I don't mince words or do performing."

And on that admission, I beamed and almost hugged that unkempt young man.

"Thank you for the biscuits," I told him.

I called my dog and made for the door.

"Livia." I turned around. "Are you alright?"

I was unable to judge his tone but my brain had an optimistic shot at his expression—soft eyes, knitted brows.

I gulped down the air.

No. Absolutely not.

I was on my metaphorical knees. Exhausted. Miserable. Anxious. Using a front of bullshit to keep me going day after day.

"Yes. Whatever makes you think I'm not?"

The balls of his cheeks raised as he winced. "Hollow eyes. Fidgeting like you're wired—and not in a good way."

Russ dropped his view to my stomach and I looked down. I was wringing my hands; frantically rubbing them, turning them inside each other. I balled my fingertips into my palms and rammed my hands into my pockets.

Shit.

He had actually seen me; for the first time, somebody had noticed the fractured woman on the inside and not the perfect, deceptive version she presented to the world.

I dropped my head, guilty as charged. Because that was me: wired, and not in a good way. Ten hours a day, fighting against the nervous fidgeting, pepped-up on cortisol and adrenaline, like an undergraduate waiting to sit their finals. Anxiety was my middle name.

"Why are you so edgy? Is it me—have I done something to scare you or summot?"

I shook my head and wiped my eyes with the back of my hand.

"I'm so tired. And there's always so much to do. Like now—tonight," I blathered; "I have to make dinner. Eat. I promised my sister I would Facetime. I've got three hours of work to get through. I won't make it to bed until after midnight and then I'll be shattered in the morning. I have a meeting at nine and I need to prepare for it beforehand and...."

"Livia. I've got this brother, Zac. One morning, when we were about fifteen, he was in the bathroom, cleaning his teeth. Stomping about. Pissed off. Argumentative. We ended up fighting—like usual—and me Dad came in and asked what was going on. Zac said I was in the way and he needed to get ready, have breakfast, phone his mate, get to school, go in detention, blah, blah.... And Dad said, calm as ought, 'Zacchary, thinking about the next ten things you've got to do has made you crazy. When you're cleaning your teeth. Just clean your teeth.'" Russ paused. "See where I'm going with this?"

I met his eye and the diagnostic tools which society had given me clanked on the floor. I didn't need to ask who he was or what he did, and I didn't need to scrutinise his clothes or credit cards to ascertain his worth. Because I could feel it. Russ was a good person. A genuine person. Somebody whose heart was in the right place.

"I think so. You think I need to stop with my mental need-to-do lists."

"There's no think about it." He smiled a tug of the lips, crinkle of the eyes, smile. "There's always a key under the second plant pot out the front. Come whenever you like. Just promise me one thing," Russ said, insistently; "leave the world at the door. No phone. No work. No thinkin' what you're having for tea. Yeah?"

I nodded and then I stood there, my arms floppy at my sides. Russ looked right back at me, his brows twitching with thought. After what seemed like a bizarre rip in the space-time continuum, he gulped down the air.

"You ever felt like somebody was important and you don't know why?" he asked pensively.

I nodded again, still staring right back at him. Absolutely. He'd hit the head on the nail I'd toyed with since the first time he looked at me in the bar. Russ felt significant. Vital. It confused me; I didn't understand.

"I ought to go. Thank you for the tea."

"Livia. When you spend your life rush, rush, rush—your mind always on the next thing—you never get the chance to enjoy what you're actually doing. Try to slow the hell down. See ya."

My foot march across the large lawn ground to an abrupt halt. Russ was right. Scarily right. And he might have well delivered the message by scud missile. Enjoyment had become something on the periphery, iridescent, and just out of reach—a condition not worthy of priority. Even when I was having a good time my mind was never focused: it whirred like a machine—a clinical, functional machine.

I thought about eating the biscuit, kicked my toes into the grass, and waited for what should ensue. Panic. Nausea. A gnarled stomach. The light-speed notions relating to every possible disconcerting reality. But those things never came. I was confused. So confused.

I walked some more and stepped onto the ancient flagstone path. I felt buoyant. Tingly. My fingers stroked the air. There was no stone in my stomach and no crazily strong gravity pulling on my legs.

Holy shit.

I was happy.

Russ said I could go back and that filled me with excitement. And I realised that the chain of negativity was absent because the neurochemicals, the endorphins, flooding my brain, were keeping the bad stuff out.

I did not just look around: I actually saw. The grass was dotted with fallen leaves. Red-brown. Ochre. The colour of burnt straw. Summer, the time for growth, was almost over and autumn was coming: dark nights and closed doors and maybe the time for renewal. Perhaps the acknowledgement of the changing seasons was because of my recent revelation. I'd always thought that life was the stage on which to strive but following Russ' comment—the one which pointed to my racing, unappreciated existence—I reasoned that to strive, strive, strive was not natural and not healthy; and perhaps to strive, reflect, and reflect some more, was the better way to go.

It was time to step back and reassess. Cut the deadwood. Delegate some more Or perhaps say 'fuck it' to it all. I could not decide.

I grinned and, with Edmund in tow, welly-ran back to my house.

Happy. Russ had made me happy. And it was a nice feeling. Really nice.

Chapter 5

Russ

"Cheer up, bruv—I'm paying tonight." Zac shoulder-barged me across the pavement. Lucky for me I was a big lad, or I'd have done face time with a tram. "And she's hot. You'll like her."

"Bet I don't," I grumbled.

My mood was dire. I wanted to be on my own, stuck in the middle of nowhere, preferably with a wall to build, a hole to dig, or something well rooted and prickly to rip from the ground. Manual labour was good for the soul.

Not that hammering, digging, or chopping was in the picture because I was walking through town on the way to the pub for the double-date my brother had talked me into. I didn't want a girlfriend and, even stranger for a bloke in his mid-twenties, I didn't even have the urge to get intimate with anybody. Well, that wasn't totally true. There was one girl, well, woman, but she was out of my league and she had some posh hunk of a boyfriend. I'd thought about her for weeks. She was beautiful—dark brown hair, a great smile, and the most amazing amber eyes. Not that I'd sleep with her given the chance. Livia was a total no-go; I was not the man for her life and she wasn't the woman for mine.

Shit.

I needed to stop thinking about her.

"I've only come to shut you up," I told my brother. "Don't try n' pimp me out, man."

Zac put his arm around my shoulder and pulled me in. "Bro, getting back in the saddle will do you good."

I shook my head, not agreeing with his suggestion. As we approached the bus stop I noticed a pack of girls eyeing us up. It was always the same when we were out together. But there was always something working against us. I looked at my brother with his trendy jeans and running shoes and I caught sight of a student in almost identical gear. The difference between them was blatantly obvious; he was from money and my brother wasn't.

Perhaps it was the hair.

The 'cool' boys had that smart hair my Mam made us have as kids because they all wanted to look like a clean-cut dude from a shit commercialised boy band. My brother didn't have a cool comb-over: he had a number two on the sides and a four on top. I just looked like I couldn't be arsed. Most days, I didn't even take the clippers to my face ne'er mind have a clean shave. But I had shaved that night and I'd tried to tidy my hair up. Yeah, I'd made a real effort: an effort to get my annoying brother off my back—he meant well but he was still a pain in the arse.

We walked into the pub and I noticed two women sitting on stools. Pretty. Slim. Long hair. Just enough make-up. I knew Zac's type. I knew they were Charlotte and Emily. Zac met Charlotte at job club, where she was a careers advisor, and he'd been out with her half-a-dozen times. I'd never met her and she was cute—as was her mate who I'd been set up with.

"Charlotte." My brother kissed her on the cheek and then lips.

Charlotte looked at him like he was a gift from god. She was deluded. She'd spill tears over him sooner or later—all of the good ones did. He only fell for girls when they were with somebody else or he was punching above his weight.

He took the stool next to her. "This is my little bruver, Russell. Russ this is Emily."

I said hello and went to the bar where I stood alone, deep in thought. Emily looked nice. She had long dark hair, blue eyes, and a cute smile. And she blushed a bit. It made her seem a bit shy and I liked that—I'd never liked pushy girls. The first time I properly met Livia she was pushy with her rah-rah posh ways and a barrage of questions but I liked her anyway. I didn't know why I liked her so much.

Five-minutes later I was approached by a spotty barman and seven minutes later I was back at the tall table with two glasses of white wine and two pints of beer, courtesy of Zac's twenty-pound note.

"Zac tells me you're a gardener, Russ?" Emily asked.

"Not quite—I'm a groundsman. I look after the estate too."

I hoped it'd stop there. But it didn't. Thankfully, our kid noticed my polite but not normal behaviour and commanded the table with his usual awe-inspiring conversation. Only joking. My brother was driven by his dick and spoke with his fists, but deep down he was a good lad and I wouldn't trade him for anybody.

As a foursome, we talked and laughed and soon Emily was climbing me like a bloody vine. We drained our glasses and Charlotte suggested we went to the bar along the road for the 'cocktails happy hour'.

I followed the others to the far corner and to a table with a long couch and a few stools. Zac and Charlotte took the back pew and I sat on a stool facing the door. Emily grabbed another and shuffled it towards mine. Zac started eating his girlfriend's face and Emily ordered us four 'Zombies'. After the drinks arrived, Zac parted terms with Charlotte and the jolly time resumed. By the time I'd drank half of the green, repulsive drink, I could ignore the girl draped around my shoulders though I was beginning to wonder if she was on the sex offenders register. My loud-mouthed, showman brother made a joke and I laughed, and then felt my smile smash on the floor.

The first couple didn't get my attention but the woman who was arm-in-arm with the next good-looking bloke did. You couldn't make it up. Same place as I first saw her. Same look on her stunning face. Livia caught my eye and her smile disappeared. She looked like she'd been slapped. I assumed it was because she didn't want to see me, in case I talked to her and cramped her style, and then I noticed the bitter glance at the girl draped around me.

I was mixed up.

All I knew was that Livia took my breath. She looked stunning in foxy heels, a pair of tight grey trousers, and a sheer shirt with a fitted vest underneath. She'd got one amazing body—slim with an arse and limbs that looked like they were sculptured by little dumbbells and lots of lunges. Her hair was different—the fringe bit pinned back in a bit of a quiff and the rest in a high ponytail. It made her look younger and less serious and, with the help of some classy, grey eye make-up, she had become the hottest woman I'd ever seen.

As Livia crossed the shiny floor to the bar, she shot me a small smile. I smiled back and downed my drink.

Zac roughly pulled my head to his. "Ya look like you've swallowed a wasp and been punched in the face. What the fuck's up wi' you?"

"Nowt. I'm fine."

Luckily, he took the hint and dropped the subject.

The waitress appeared and Zac ordered another round of random cocktails. I was totally off kilter and, in spite of been half-baked already, I decided to drink my way through it. I tried not to see her. I tried not to look at her because of him. I didn't know whether he was her boyfriend or fiancé but he looked too good to be true. The bloke had the sort of face they put on aftershave adverts. He was tall, broad, and dressed in well-cut jeans and a navy V-necked sweater with a white and blue checked shirt underneath. God, I hated him and his smugness and his fucking charm. Livia didn't look charmed—she looked even more off kilter than I felt. I could no longer ignore the girl whose hand was on my thigh. I wanted to shove her off.

Livia tottered towards the toilets, as good as falling over her feet. I followed two seconds later and was through the door and into the corridor just after her. She turned sharply and then, with the heels of her palms in her eye sockets, she shook her head over and over.

"Livia. What's up?" I asked, touching the top of her arm.

She turned away from me and said nothing. Her shoulders were shaking. She was crying.

"Livia, babe."

I had no idea why I called her babe and or why I grabbed her arm and ushered her into the disabled toilet. Red emergency cords. Bright white light. A load of screwed up toilet roll in the corner. A toilet which smelled a bit iffy.

Bloody hell.

Some blokes whisked the woman of their dreams to Paris or Rome or a candlelit restaurant—but not me—I took mine to a toilet cubicle—complete with sanitary bin and splash pad in front of the pan. I wasn't holding out for five stars on Trip Advisor.

I closed the door and pulled the silver lever to seal us in. I could hear her sobs because the bar noise was muted.

I peeled the hands from her face. "Why the hell are you crying?"

"I'm just pissed."

Her words were almost hidden by the sound of water squeezing through the pipes. Going someplace else. To wash somebody else's hands clean. To flush somebody else's mess away. I dragged my thumb up her cheek and wiped away her tears.

"Being pissed shouldn't make you cry. It should make you happy."

"You didn't look too happy when your girlfriend was as good as licking your face," she snapped. "I'm sorry. I shouldn't have said that."

"She's not my girlfriend. I landed her on a double date. I thought she was nice at first but I'm starting to wonder if she's the local sex offender. Either that or it's the freekin Lynx effect—I knew I should have used some of my Dad's Brut instead," I joked.

Livia pulled her trembling lips into a tiny smile. I moved the thumb from her cheek and put a kiss in its place. I thought Livia would tell me off, shove me, or start giving reasons why I shouldn't have pushed her into the toilet and kissed her. But she didn't. There was wanting in those amber eyes of hers and I tipped her face by the chin and touched her mouth with mine. I didn't really kiss her. I waited till she kissed me and then the girl rocked my world. Salty tears. Lip gloss. And then she sucked my bottom lip and, not only was I hard, but I was mentally on my knees.

I was fucked. Absolutely fucked.

I touched her face, spreading my fingers around her dainty jaw and into the back of her hair. I struggled to breathe. Livia pulled me away from her with a tug on my hair.

"Let's go, Russ. Come home with me. Please."

Her fingers ran along my shaven cheek and she followed them with her eyes—studying me. I'd never wanted to do anything more in my whole life. We could go back to the corridor and leave by the fire escape. I could phone Zac and say I'd thrown up and he would make my excuses. But I couldn't. If I got involved with her my life would, yet again, resemble a zombie with leprosy. Wandering. Aimless. Bits dropping off everywhere. Struggling to keep it together.

"I can't, Livia." I hardly got the words out before she kissed me again; I pulled her away. The rich-poor divide was too massive—it couldn't work.

"You need to go back to the rich guy. You can't just leave him at the table." She looked at her shoes and the tears started to build again. "Babe, stop crying. You're pissed. You don't know what you're sayin'. Take a deep breath, go back in there, and get a packet of crisps to soak up the wine."

I dried her tears again, kissed her on the forehead, and reluctantly left that beige tiled cubicle. I wanted her—god I did—but letting her close probably equated to me marching up to the alter reserved for human sacrifices. No shit. My thoughts were bipolar: run from her—take her home—there were equal odds on me pushing her under a car or asking her to marry me the next time we met.

Luckily, Zac was sitting at the bar and I went to his side—unable to face the strangers at the table without him. He peered at me out of the corner of his eye. I said nothing and stared ahead. The barman went to him.

"Four of them Green Goblins please." The barman headed off and I felt Zac's stare on my face. "Firstly T, you look like you've been dragged through a bush. Secondly, the person who put you through it was wearing lipstick. And lastly, are you shagging that rich bloke's missus?"

That bloody brother of mine. He didn't miss a trick—just like me and Dad. I smoothed my hair with my palms, rubbed at my mouth with the back of my hand, and glanced at the dark pink on my skin.

"Has it gone?"

"Yeah. Now, how long 'av you been screwing the posh bird?"

I shook my head. "I'm not. I kind of work for 'er. She lives at the manor."

"Whoo, hoo," my brother said, joyously. "Her husband's gonna flip when he finds out you are giving her one. You dirty, lucky—"

His words halted as Livia's partner appeared beside me. He was not happy, but neither was I, and if he started I'd batter him.

The guy curled his hands around the bar. "What have you done you little scum bag?"

"Excuse me?" I snapped, offended.

I glared at my brother. I could sense his aggression and I didn't need him to fight my battles. The rich guy squared up his jaw and stared me in the eye.

"The lady accompanying me left the bar to visit the ladies'. You followed shortly after and she came back ten minutes later having obviously been crying. Have you threatened her? Accosted her?"

My mouth dropped open. Offended didn't come close.

"No," I replied, and took a drink of the concoction which had appeared in front of me.

"I don't believe you, you arrogant chav. Why the hell would she be crying?" he spat. "I'm calling the police. You can tell them what you did."

Livia suddenly appeared—we were making a scene.

"Just leave it, Kieran."

She was back using her 'rah rah' voice. It grated on me and I was glad she didn't use it when we were alone.

The guy shook his head. "No. I will not leave it, Olivia. A lady should be able to visit the bathroom without being reduced to tears by some youth."

I didn't like his tone and I didn't like him bossing her. "Don't talk to her like that."

"Who the fuck are you to be taking that tone with me? I'm having you thrown out of here."

He raised his hand to summon the barman and I raised mine to warm my agitated brother to sit down and keep his hands in his pockets.

"He's done nothing wrong. Just leave it, Kieran," she as good as pleaded. "He's my friend."

The man, who I knew to be Kieran, looked at me, disgusted. "Your friend, Livia! Where the hell have you met somebody like him?"

Like me! I assumed he wasn't referring to hardworking, well-mannered, and reasonably educated. I assumed he was referring to the fact I wasn't affluent, drank beer instead of prosecco, and wore trainers. Regardless, he wasn't happy about his girlfriend talking to me.

"At home. He's the gardener and stop being such a fucking arse," she said, angrily. "I'm a big girl and I don't need you puffing your chest out like a fucking superhero."

"Stop swearing," he snapped; "it doesn't become you."

"And what am I?" she returned.

It was apparent me and Zac were about to witness a domestic—that was if one of us didn't snap and turn it into a brawl. It was touch and go. If he

35

spoke to her like that again I'd lose it and if my brother looked any more hostile I would have to hit him to save him from himself.

"You're just a little drunk, honey. Come on let's go home."

And with that, he glowered at me and pulled on her arm. She touched my hand, resting her slender, soft finger against my thick, calloused thumb. It was one finger and one thumb but it said everything. Livia, her life privileged and sterile, and me, toughened and stained by my existence. We were poles apart and it would never work. Even if I could get over all of my personal shit, we could never work. Probably, as tempted as I was, not even the once. I felt like she wanted me to stand up and take her away from everything. But that was crazy and I was pissed and my head was still in a spin after kissing her in that toilet. I said nothing. Of course, I said nothing. I let her go back to her rah-rah friends with her super smooth boyfriend. I left her in her privileged little world because I'd never be anything to her.

I needed to get the taste of Livia out of my mouth; I needed her out of my head and probably my life. I knew I should go back to the table, drink that drink, and snog the pretty girl who'd been all over me all night. But I didn't. I made my polite excuses and went home—angry and bitter that he was with her and I had let it happen. If I carried on with the insanity I would be totally fucked. It would be far worse than last time; far, far, worse than last time.

Chapter 6

Livia

I was frantic. I searched the house top to bottom, checked out the communal areas, and ran around the entire garden numerous times. I had no idea where he was and no idea how he'd got out, but Edmund was gone. I decided to head back to the house and leave the doors open in a hope my dog would come back of his own accord.

My hands shook as I poured the umpteenth coffee of the day; I could feel the tightening and pulsing of anxiety inside. There were times when my blood did not feel my own— it coursed in my veins and, rather than deliver sustenance, it made me light-headed, weak, and vacant. The only thing that seemed to abate the anxiety was running or wine and I was definitely doing too much of both. The herbal stuff was not working and I'd started to suffer from heartburn when I was feeling really wound up. And I was wound up so I washed a few Rennies down with the coffee.

Rather than put some crap on the telly and calm down, I turned on my iPad and typed in 'dog thefts in The Midlands'. I soon wished that I hadn't. The first link to appear was about the circulation of an Eastern European gang which was operating in suburbia and stealing pedigree dogs from gardens.

My old rational mind would have reasoned that the chances of a white van pulling up, unnoticed, and snatching the only dog from a walled garden were very remote. But I no longer had my old mind. Mine was corrupted and the worse-case scenario was my response to everything. The concept of somebody taking my dog was too much to bear and I sat and cried as I drank my coffee. I knew it had happened because I'd done something I shouldn't have: I'd broken one of my rules.

I was cramming my feet into my trainers, the tears streaming down my face, when I heard a light rapping coming from the front door—the one fed from the shared foyer. Cursing at the distraction, I kicked off my shoes and stomped to the other door. First, I saw the ruddy blonde-haired man and then I saw my dog, which, the second he was released at the collar, came running to me, his claws making his feet flail from under him on my polished wooden floor.

"Bloody hell, Edmund, where have you been?" I sobbed, burying my face into his wet, smelly fur.

"In the lake."

I averted my eyes and became fully aware of Russ—the man who had kissed me and who was consuming most of my waking thoughts. He was standing in stocking feet, a wet jumper, and no trousers.

"Oh gosh, you're wet too!" I exclaimed. "Please come in. Thank you for finding him. Did you say lake?"

I stepped away from the door and he squelched inside.

"Yep. He's lucky I was down there feedin' my chickens. He couldn't get out cos the bank was too steep."

"But how did he get out of the garden?"

"There's a dug-out in the far corner. I dunno if it's foxes or badgers but as fast as I fill it in they'll scoop it back out. I'll get some chicken wire and dig it in."

I held up a cup and my coffee pot to offer him a drink. Looking uneasy, he offered a polite 'no ta', and then I blathered and blathered and almost insisted.

"Oh, go on then—don't suppose one would hurt."

I looked down at his semi-clad state and the soft blond hair on his legs. He had good legs—very good legs—nicely muscular, like a footballer, I thought. I blushed. What was I thinking. "Would you like me to put your stuff in the tumble drier and where are your trousers and shoes?"

"The front door step. I've been brought up better than to walk water and mud into other people's houses."

"Please," I flustered, "go and get them and I'll dry the lot. I could lend you something till they're dry."

"Cheers."

"Erm, clothes," I pondered, scratched my head, and gestured for him to follow me to my bedroom.

I sifted through my wardrobe but the biggest thing I could find was a white fluffy dressing gown.

My day was not going to plan, though, to be fair, my life went off course the first time I saw him. And well, after what happened in the bar, I had started to dream and think just maybe. He'd never seemed interested before but then he kissed me and I was very confused.

He chuckled a little and shook his head. "What about a towel?"

"Oh yes. Have a shower too if you like."

I directed him to my en-suite, handed him a large clean towel, and hurried back to the kitchen to be reunited with my naughty dog before my mind lost a grip of my senses.

Russ

Nobody appreciates how good it is to stand in a warm bathroom unless they usually stand in a freezing one. Our bathroom was always draughty because we needed to leave the window open to keep the damp down. And when you were in the shower and our kid burst in, the shower curtain sucked in and stuck on you like a cold, wet bin liner. Nasty.

In Livia's bathroom, everything was warm. The floor. The twisted chrome radiators. And the water was hot—at home, the first person got the hot water, the second the warm, and the last had to be in and out before the hypothermia set in—the joys of a hot water tank—one day I'd buy me Mam and Dad a combi-boiler.

The bathroom took me from my world and dumped me in one where the sharp corners were sanded smooth and the soft lighting hid the cracks and grime. Just like Livia did. She took me away from the grey of my reality. Hot as hell and just posh enough for it to be horny, but vulnerable and kind of nice to be with. Not that I was going there. Kissing her was a very stupid thing to do—she was on the opposite end of the social spectrum and she had a boyfriend. Well, I assumed he was her boyfriend because she didn't wear an engagement ring, but he was still one lucky bastard to have her.

The shower cubicle was massive with one of those big round shower-heads that come from the ceiling and, like, rain on you, and a curved glass screen to keep the splashes in. There was another shower head in a holder on the tap and nozzles set into the wall, but I wasn't going to start pulling levers and turning dials to get them going.

If it wasn't for the woman outside I could have stayed in there all day, but a squirt of some frothy, perfumed, shower wash later, and I was clean. Smelling like a woman, but clean. Clean on the outside anyway—the lake water I'd swallowed was vile but it couldn't be as dirty as the thoughts in my head.

I turned off the water and dried myself using her fluffy towel. I looked at my boxer shorts on the floor, all screwed up and soggy, and decided to go commando—putting those things on would be grim. My eyes continued to roam; there was a neat line of women's potions on a glass shelf and a little basket of cotton wool balls on the counter. But there was one toothbrush in the holder and no man's toiletries anywhere—no shower gel, no deodorant or razor. My mind wandered. Perhaps the boyfriend wasn't that serious. I didn't know why I cared anyway. The woman was right out of my league. I wrapped the towel around my waist, hoped Livia wasn't easily offended, and left the sanctuary of the bathroom.

Livia

My life was no longer in tatters. My dog was back in the fold and there was a half-naked man in my kitchen who made me happier than a pig in shit. It was not his body, though by god it helped, it was his calmness—his simplicity. Russ was a humble person who followed his instincts and did; he did not spend time pondering over his words, considering his actions, and applying layer after layer of socially expected strata before he presented a carefully constructed person to the world. And in my frame of mind, that realisation made him even more enticing.

I pushed out a stool and pointed to the cup. He sat beside me, pulling down the towel to cover the seat and offering me an accidental flash in the process.

"Sorry babe," he uttered, through a grin.

I laughed the first laugh in days.

Babe! I could not believe he had called me babe again and I found it funny. From anybody else the term would be condescending but with him it seemed endearing.

I glanced past his shoulders and to the soft hairs on his swelling chest muscles; his view remained firmly on his hands.

"Don't worry about it, babe," I teased. "Perving at you in that towel is only one of two good things that've happened all day—the other being the appearance of my dog by the way."

Russ laughed, deep and bawdily. "I'm not sure you should be commenting on another bloke's tackle. I don't think your boyfriend would be 'appy."

"Boyfriend?"

"Yeah the have-a-go-hero from the other night. The bloke who turns up in a posh black car and takes you out."

"No. No," I said, "he's, erm, one of my hired helpers."

Russ looked at me, properly, for the first time since he came in the room.

"My hired helpers! Well, golly gosh m' lady," he mocked. "So he's a gigolo?"

"An escort—it's not quite the same."

"Fuck me!" he exclaimed. "How many people does it take to scratch your itch?"

I coloured up at his coarseness but he did not offend me.

"No. Not to scratch my itch. Kieran accompanies me socially and erm," *and moving swiftly on,* "the cleaner cleans my house, the personal trainer makes me exercise, the gardener…"

"What does the gardener do?" He glanced at my lips and then back at my eyes.

"He tends to the garden," I replied, chewing my lip.

Russ twiddled his thumbs and watched them, scowling. He was uneasy in my company. "Do you actually pay that bloke to get in you?" he asked in disbelief.

I looked at my hands. "Not exactly."

"He's bored you know," Russ said, blatantly redirecting the subject.

"Who? Kieran?"

"No, the dog. He's cooped up in 'ere all day. I'm not surprised he did a runner."

I started to cry again. That little comment nearly buried me in remorse. I knew Edmund was feeling the neglect due to my frantic career as much as I and his attempt at suicide was probably a cry for help. Russ tapped me sympathetically on the hand. I really wanted him to hug me or kiss me again but he was detached and closed and I knew touching me was gesture enough.

"It was my fault." I could not believe what I was about to say. "I ran five miles this morning."

"And?"

"Well, I always run four, six, eight, or something. But after I ate the biscuit and nothing bad happened I felt brave enough to try an odd number. So, I did and I made this happen." I could hear the cogs turning in his head and I knew he must think I'd escaped from the local asylum.

"Livia," he said, flatly, "it was your fault the dog got out. You made it happen because you never shut the door. It has nowt to do with running an odd number of miles."

"But it does," I twittered. "If I don't do the things I need to do it makes bad things happen and…"

Russ stopped my words with a soft look and a shake of the head.

"Babe, your mind is kicking out and making you think that shit. If you don't want to crash the car, mess up at work, or leave the door open and lose the dog, give your mind a break. Turn off your phone and computer at five, go to bed at ten-thirty, and abandon the stupidly early mornings."

"But I need to get up so early," I returned. "I have to wash, do my makeup, go for my morning run—with Edmund of course—eat, shower, get dressed, blow-dry my hair, do my makeup…"

"Why the hell do you put on makeup before you go for a run?"

My cheeks suddenly felt hot, very hot. "I might bump into somebody and I don't want them commenting behind my back and, such as today, I've got a spot on my chin so I could never leave home without hiding it."

"Where's the spot?"

I pointed at the offending article and grimaced.

"Livia, you're a beautiful woman…"

Then, much to my surprise, Russ rubbed the powder, foundation and concealer from my spot and I let him.

"Now you're a beautiful woman with a spot on her chin. You could wash all of that makeup away and you'd still be a beautiful woman with a spot on her chin. You are who you are, Livia, and people who aren't prepared to take you for who you are don't deserve your time. See my point?"

I smiled—I couldn't help it.

"And if you want to be even more beautiful, do a bit more of that," he told me, referring to my grin. "The chemicals in your brain get unbalanced when you don't get enough sleep, don't laugh, and don't have enough orgasms," he continued. "Oh, and chocolate is meant to work for girls an' all."

"I'm not really that bothered about chocolate."

"So what do you like? What makes you happy?"

I looked at him and the darkness bombed in. He was the only person who had made me properly happy in ages—letting me in his hut and kissing me in the bar. But he was not mine and that made me sad and I started to cry again.

"I'm sorry. Perhaps you should go. I'm such an embarrassment."

And I really felt like it—spewing my weird thoughts to him and then hiding my red, weepy eyes.

"What's with all the crying, Livia?"

"I feel bad about shutting him in here all day. I'll get a dog-sitter."

He paused, contemplating, mulling things over. "He can mooch 'bout around here with me I s'pose. I like dogs and I don't like the thought of forcing living things into boxes...rabbits in cages, people in offices, dogs in houses..."

"Would you? Would you really? I'll give you a key so you can take him out and bring him back as you please. It would be great, it really would."

And I'd get an excuse to see you.

"As you wish m' lady. Though you might not thank me if he goes in that bloody lake again cos I'll leave him to drown."

I smiled; I really smiled and then blew my nose. He'd rescued Edmund, cheered me up, and then offered to keep my dog company so he didn't fall into a depression like me. I wanted Russ to stay longer but he didn't. He got his damp clothes out of the tumble drier, reluctantly took the spare key, said goodbye, and left me marooned.

And so, the relationship between Russ and my dog began. Sometimes he came for him before I left for work and sometimes he came later. Often, I would arrive home and find Edmund hot on his heels in the garden, or curled up waiting at the bottom of a ladder while he tended to maintenance around the hall. Much to my disappointment I was never included, and on the days I retrieved Edmund from Russ' domain it was a civilised handover like a child between divorced parents. It was very much a case of two's company and three's a crowd.

And crazily, every bit of distance he put between us and every word he never said made me want him more. Each day I left the bland, styled people in my business world—those who were cleaned of their earthliness and considered their words—and gleefully went home in anticipation of a possible minute with a man who dug the ground, ate a cheese sandwich with grubby hands, and who restrained his thoughts like they were the secret which could end the world.

Chapter 7

Livia

On the advice from my friend Ellie, I happily took some time off work to join her for a bite to eat and a drink. She was going through a rough time and needed a good laugh, and rightly pointed out, 'you used to be exciting but now you're as dull as fuck'.

We started by stuffing ourselves senseless in Nando's before going to the pub. By four o'clock we were steaming; by half-past we were trying to remain upright on the train back home; by five I struggled to remember my address to tell the cab driver. Ellie was going home with me and her friend was collecting her on her commute from work.

"Where's the smelly mutt?" Ellie joked, as we fell inside my house.

"He doesn't smell, it's just his breath and, oh my, wait until you see who shares custody of him now." I could not believe I had been drunk and disorderly for so long and not mentioned my compulsive, addictive obsession with the groundskeeper. "Shut that door and follow me."

Ellie, giggling like a child on a bear hunt, followed me on my usual path of discovery: across the main lawn, past the box-hedge maze, along the edge of the new salad and herb garden, and towards the stone shed tucked away from prying eyes.

I knew if I did not see them en route they would be in the hut, where Russ, like a right little Alan Titchmarsh, would end the day sharpening his spade, oiling his shears, and doing the things I thought people no longer cared about in our disposable society.

I tapped lightly on the aged-to-silver wooden door and a reserved voice told me to come in. He knew it was me because Edmund was wagging his tail; I could hear it banging on something wooden.

I peered inside and gingerly entered. "Hi."

"Ah m' lady."

On the rare occasion he was in the mood for a limited conversation he always called me babe or m' lady—a piss-take of me living in the manor.

Russ looked at me wearing a smothered grin and, after rubbing my dog's head, I put my hands on my hips.

"What is that look for and what on earth are you doing?"

He was on his hands and knees in the very old fireplace, looking up the chimney while poking it with a stick.

"Tryin' to unblock this chimney. Winter's comin' and it's stupid having the heater on when there's wood everywhere." There was a brief pause. "Ed, will you shift. If you get covered in soot I'm chucking you back in that lake."

The dog raised a distinctive eyebrow and returned to my feet. I could not be sure whether it was Russ' tone or my dog's exceptional grasp of the English language, but it appeared that Edmund understood Russ as well as he did me. I only wished I understood Russ as well as my dog did.

"This is my friend, Ellie."

Russ turned briefly, raised a hand, said hello, and asked me if I was 'pissed'. I told him I was and he smiled. Yes. It appeared he was well and truly in his own little world.

"Come on Edmund, let's go. We'll leave the talkative chimney sweep to it," I said, the sarcasm dripping.

A chuckle emanated from the cavity of the small chimney breast. "Nice to meet you, Ellie."

I took heed of my friend's inquisitive expression and gestured for her to walk through the door.

"See you tomorrow, Russ. Thanks for looking after the dog."

"No problem m' lady."

I had managed two steps before a bang and a string of expletives exploded out of the stone building. I quickly back-tracked and burst in just in time to see Russ stand up, shake his head, and use the bottom of his t-shirt to wipe his face. And yes, I was looking at the flat, honey-coloured stomach he flashed in the process. I took an amused look at his blackened face, dust-caked hair and filthy clothes.

"It looks like you better get back in my shower. I hope you've got spare clothes in the car this time."

He shook his head and tried to get some of the dust out of his eyes. "Nah, I've not even got the car anymore. I hope you've got a bigger towel."

I grinned. I was drunk and feeling leery. "No, today's towel will be even smaller. You can wash the thick off in the shower and have a soak in my bath. It'll take twenty minutes to run."

I stopped his protests with a playful glare.

"Thank you," he returned. "I'll get the chickens in and lock up."

Ellie threaded her arm through mine and we weaved up the path as my dog repeatedly shoved his slimy nose in my free hand. I interpreted her silence as questioning and with a fake huff asked 'what?'

"You're so dirty! I can't believe you're living out some Lady Chatterley fantasy with your gardener. My lady! Ha ha ha," she laughed.

"Ellie, I've never even read the book. All I know is it's about some rich woman who shagged the gardener and it caused a right uproar because of the sex."

"It didn't only cause an uproar because of the sex. It caused an uproar because the sex was between an upper-class woman and a lower-class man!"

"Oh." The discussion was not one which I wanted; sex was no longer a taboo subject but inter-class relations were still frowned upon. "He calls me m' lady because he's poking fun. That's all. No smut. No scandal. Sorry."

She looked at me in shock. "No way, you really aren't shagging him!"

"No! I wish I was but I don't think he fancies me. Some days he hardly says two words."

Ellie cocked her head and raised an eyebrow. "He so does fancy you and I am downloading the book onto your iPad as soon as we get in."

"Whatever," I groaned.

After arriving home, the first job was to dish out a large bowl of crunchy dog mix for Edmund, the next to set the bath running, and the last to phone for a couple of pizzas. Ellie would be going after carrying out her literary task and I was hoping to lure Russ into staying for a while after his bath.

I made my machinations as Ellie and I chatted; Russ' clothes would need washing and, as such, I reckoned I could keep him for up to two hours. I was tipsy, ragingly hormonal, and looking forward to feasting my eyes on his lithe body.

Russ turned up, trousers in hand, as we were about to head out to the front gates—Ellie for her lift and me for the takeaway. I twiddled the knob and pressed a few buttons on the washer and told Russ to throw his clothes in before he got in the bath. He grinned dryly at my bossiness and offered his usual zero-word response. Ellie said goodbye and we headed down the drive to the gates.

Half way down the gravelled road, I rubbed my hands together and grinned like a child. "I'm in for a good perv tonight, Ell. I swear if it wasn't for him I'd disappear into a pit of despair."

"Is Kieran not doing it for you anymore, Liv?"

I thought for a moment. "No, I don't think he ever really did. Anyway, clocking a look at Russell tonight is gonna set me up for the week! Kieran is personal trainer sculptured, smooth and perfect, but I'm not sure I want that any more. Russ is natural and he's not all chiselled and vain— though his arms and shoulders look like he does weights." *Hmmm.* "Oh and he's a bit hairy. Like an untamed, feral beast. God, I want him."

Ellie pointed along the road as her friend's Toyota came into view. "I think you should give it a go. You've lost your mojo, honey," she said, pulling me into a hug, "and a good seeing to will do you good."

Yes. That was my line and she'd just pinched it.

I opened a bottle of Chateau Neuf and was ripping into my new story as Russ sauntered into my kitchen wearing a smile and a white fluffy towel. I asked him if he wanted a drink and he politely declined, citing the reasons he was not really keen on wine and needed to cycle home. And so, firing on all barrels, I produced a large bottle of Peroni and then nodded to the illuminated oven in which two cardboard pizza boxes were keeping warm.

And that was all of the persuasion it required.

Four slices of farmhouse pizza and two bottles of beer later, he had offered me smiles but not many words.

"Why don't you like me anymore, Russ?" I asked, the wine providing my courage.

He looked at me like I'd just dropped my skirt and pulled a moon.

"I do."

"Then why don't you talk to me and why do you avoid me?"

Russ placed his elbows on the table. "Cos' I fancy you like fuck. I want to keep my distance."

There was no beating around the bush with him when he actually decided to talk.

I gulped down the air. "Why would you do that? I don't see the issue."

I reached under the island for another beer and pushed it to him. I wanted to hear more.

"Even if I had a chance with you I'd run a mile. I don't want to be involved with anybody. And I fancy you because you're as hot as hell... I like your hands and your lips are made for sucking cocks."

I recharged with wine and pizza. "I fancy you 'like fuck' too."

"No you don't, you're just pissed."

"Yes, I do. Because you're crafted by hard work and you are unpolished and I want you to make me feel real. No suits. No shaving. No playing with words. I want to lie on that rug," I pointed to the wool offering in front of the central wood burner, "and hitch up my skirt, and I want you to fuck me with none of the pretentious bullshit that is my life and with the earthly goodness that is yours."

He looked at his hands, shaking his head. "No Livia."

"Why?"

"Because you'll hate me for it after. Men like me don't do things like that to women like you."

I reached over to touch his hand and he flinched—like I'd burned him.

"I won't hate you. And what 'is a woman like me' anyway?"

"One who would be shamed if she shagged a scruffy gardener outside her little circle of privilege. You know what they'd say about you."

"I couldn't give a fuck."

"When the girls 'round me say fuck they sound thick. When a posh woman like you says it, you sound dirty. It's really erotic."

"Are you hard?" Grinning, he shook his head. I tugged at the edge of the towel. "Oh fuck. Semi-hard by the looks of it— but I reckon ten seconds with these cock-sucking lips..."

"Stop it, Livia."

I stood up and rushed towards him and Russ jumped away like I was the local leper. He was in front of the washer-drier before I had time to blink, pulling his nearly dry clothes from out of the drum and dressing like a man possessed. Avoiding my eye completely, he muttered that he needed to go and rushed to the scratchy mat by the door to collect his shoes. I stood, mouth agape, at his blatant rejection and then stared in disbelief as Edmund raced through from his basket in the hall—his legs flailing in excitement. My dog sat at Russ' feet, peered at him with those spooky blue eyes, and bashed the floor with his tail. He had chosen to go with him rather than stay with me and that gesture, along with rejection and several glasses of wine, brought my world crashing down.

I was a stone; I was a rock covered in sediment and slime; trying to shine and trying to stay on the shore while I got dragged further and further into the murky depths by the tide.

I could have shrugged off the fact I had been blatantly rejected by the man I'd wanted for weeks and got my kicks from the rabbit sitting in my bedside drawer; I could have taken a deep breath and told my dog he could play with Russ tomorrow; but my tormented, modern brain could take no more and I went back to the stool, dropped my face into my hands, and cried. For the eighteenth consecutive day, I was shedding tears. My actions were neither manipulative nor purposeful. The loss of Edmund's faithfulness was more than I could take.

"I'm sorry," I muttered. "You need to go. I'm only upset because my dog likes you more than me."

He touched my arm but I didn't look up through my shame, instead I reached down to pat the soft, guilty face which dropped on my thigh—the dog that was—not the man.

"He doesn't—he thinks I'm taking him out. Don't cry. Please babe. Don't cry. You've got nothing to be miserable about. Beautiful, wicked dog, nice house, good job...."

The lightly calloused hand traced a path from my wrist to my elbow.

"Ignore me and go home." I smiled thinly. "I always cry. I'm not trying to make you feel bad."

"Why do you always cry?"

I shrugged and realised his hand was circling my shoulder. "It's just what I do."

And then a soft kiss landed on my cheek, blotting a tear away. "There. Better."

I smiled again and squeezed his hand. "Ride carefully. I'll probably see you tomorrow."

I gestured for him to shoo and then noticed the fingers of my other hand were curled around his. He stared at them intently.

"Promise you won't cry tomorro' and I'll shag you on the rug."

I laughed; I could not believe his forthrightness.

"I've not cried to make you shag me because you feel sorry for me."

"I don't feel sorry for you. I thought if I could make it to the door I'd get away."

He pulled on my hand, told Edmund to go back to the hall, and led me to the rug in front of the wood burner. And still weeping a little, half-pissed, and lusting like a teenager, I stood there and waited for him to do something.

Russ appeared unsure and apprehensive. He rummaged in his pocket and produced his wallet which he threw on the floor as he started to undo the buttons on my silk blouse. I halted the progress of his fingers, reached under my skirt, pulled down my knickers and kicked them off my feet.

"No romance, no bullshit, Russ. I just want you in me."

I meant every word. I'd had boyfriend after boyfriend who wined, dined, and seduced me; slow undressing, bodily kisses, and the layering of expected ritual that led to the most basal of acts. I didn't want that; I wanted the act without the stage; I wanted things to be different with him. I told him these thoughts and, with a puzzled stare and his brows knitted together, he asked me again if I was sure I wanted to be intimate with a minimum wage gardener who didn't even have a working car. I told him again that I did, bashfully lay on the rug, and propped myself on my elbows as I watched him undo his trousers. And then he stopped, knelt in front of me, and pulled me to my knees. Russ studied my mouth and then wetted his lips. He ran his hands up my thighs, watching them as he did. I placed my hands on his hands. Hell, I was nervous.

"You never kissed anybody before?" he teased.

I clearly looked as nervous as I felt.

"There was this one guy—in a toilet in a bar," I returned, my cheeks flushed. "Have you ever kissed anybody before?"

"Hmmm. There was this one girl—in a toilet in a bar."

I swallowed. The butterflies rioted in my tummy. I was right there, back before my very first kiss and, judging by his expression, so was he. Russ placed his palm on my cheek and ran his thumb along my lip.

"Yeah," he continued, his voice scratchy; "and I'm gonna kiss her again."

I ran my tongue along my lips and closed my eyes. Russ stroked his lips across mine and I wanted to drag air into my lungs like I'd just sprinted up a hill.

Shit.

His hand was in the back of my hair and my hand was under his t-shirt. Soft skin.

A scattering of hair.

I'd changed my mind about a semi-clothed fuck on the rug. I didn't even care if we had sex—I'd be happy to kiss him for the rest of my life. I clambered onto his lap and he kicked his legs out straight, holding me tight so I didn't end up on my backside. I giggled. He smiled against my lips and pulled me close. I pressed against him and changed my mind about the sex. I needed him in me and I told him so. I fought to get a hand into his jeans before he lowered me on the rug and there I lay, brazen as anything, with my legs akimbo and my skirt around my waist as I watched him tend to the contraception. I had never felt hornier. There was no bullshit and no pretence. He lowered his body onto mine and again tried to cajole me with foreplay, before I took a firm hold of his buttocks and pulled him right into my wanton body. *Holy shit.*

My floppy arms slapped by my sides. Sex had never been like that and it had never felt so good. I was lost: absolutely lost in him— intoxicated by lust and disbelief. I told him to come and he uttered in protest and started to touch me. For the first time in my life I was not under a man for a climax— I was under him for his. I wanted to feel like we were here because of his desire and not because of my coercion. I wanted him to claim me. I needed him to hold me and kiss me and make me feel like he would never let me go. Russ rolled onto the carpet and pulled me on to him. He kissed my head and stroked tiny circles on the top of my arm.

"Are you going to hate me now?"

Dizzied by what had just happened, I shook my head. "No." Admittedly, I was feeling a little disjointed following our impromptu joining and separation but there was no bitterness. "Are you going to hate me?"

"No. Course not."

"Thank you."

He blew out through his nose and smiled. "Don't be silly, babe—you don't have to thank me. Now, no crying tomorrow." He kissed my temple and wriggled from my clutches. "But I really need to go. Those two beers are gonna make me slow enough as it is."

I nodded and made myself tidy; he got up and adjusted his attire.

"I'll see you tomorrow."

And with that, I got a bashful smile and he left.

Chapter 8

Russ

"Are you going to hate me now?" she asked me.

"No. Course not," I replied.

Though hating her would never be the problem: it was loving her which could be the tetanus-ridden, serrated knife in my side. And loving her was a real possibility. I knew it the second I saw her in that bar. I knew it when I first kissed her. I knew it when she flitted around my hut, nervous and bumbling like a freekin bee. Quirky. Fragile. A whole lot deeper than she appeared—and messed up—totally bloody screwy.

My mind churned as my heavy legs forced the pedals down over and over; I wished I'd got more money and more resistance.

I didn't want money for posh clothes or fancy meals: I wanted to fix my car so I wasn't cycling a twenty-five-mile round trip to work each day. I'd been paid but all of my spare money went into buying my Mam a new washer; her old one wouldn't spin and I couldn't stand seeing her wring out the clothes by hand. There were another twenty-two days 'til pay day and then I could get a new clutch. With any luck, me and my bro could fit it and I could get enough life out of the banger to get me through winter.

As for the resistance. I'd given in and had sex with Livia. I shouldn't have done it. It wasn't those sad eyes or those tears—it was that little hand of hers, curled around mine. A hand almost told as much as a face and she kept clinging to me without realising it. Those hands told of her rank in the social circus; still brown from a foreign holiday, soft and smooth because she paid somebody else to dirty their hands for her. My hands had a band of thick, rough skin at the top of my palm and my fingers were ingrained with dirt that never came off never mind how much I scrubbed. The sight of her hand wrapped around mine pushed me too far. It silently proved she was out of my league and that made her so much more tempting.

Dangerous and tempting.

Livia asked me to 'fuck' her. It was obvious, harsh and blatant, that I was a bit of rough in her sparkling world. I was a knee-jerk reaction to the shit in her head.

Transient.

Disposable.

But I had been messed about and punished enough.

I needed to keep my head and so I decided to keep out of her way.

Just to be sure.

Chapter 9

Livia

Investment portfolio.

Offshore immunity.

Shares.

Hedge fund.

The words of the morning were nothing but an annoying distraction. At one point, I nearly faked sickness and left the boardroom—which was ironic really—the day before I nearly left due to an anxiety-induced panic attack. All I could think about was him; the contemplative look on his face as he dropped on the floor between my legs; the touch of his scratchy hand; his lips on mine; him inside….

"Livia."

A curt voice distracted me from my naughty thoughts.

"Sorry Garvin, yes, absolutely," I returned, my immediate grasp of the conversation implying my ears were open in spite of my mind been elsewhere. "As I listed in the proposal, I recommend a thirty percent allocation as a maximum—given the market instability it would be prudent to maintain a substantial liquid reserve."

The men around the table nodded in unison and I wrapped up the meeting with a summarising of points, an apportionment of tasks, and a polite 'excuse me'. I needed to get back to my office, top up on caffeine, ramp up my air conditioning, and get my mind back on the job.

"Is everything okay, Livia?" my assistant, Elizabeth, asked as she placed a coffee in front of me.

"Yes," I lied; "what makes you ask?"

"Well," she started, "you seem very absent-minded today and you've lost weight of late."

Elizabeth had worked for me for years and embarrassingly I was closer to her than my friends and family. Though still I could not talk to her. The veneer of coping was established and strengthened with the bastions of expectation. Nobody knew of my failings or saw my daily tears: nobody except Russ. I smiled broadly, pushed the glasses from the bridge of my nose, and rested them in my hair.

"I'm absolutely fine. I suppose the wine session with Ellie has caught up on me. I keep forgetting I'm not twenty any longer."

My performance was exemplary and she had no clue that I was questioning the reason for everything. All I could think of was Russ and how my world had been coloured in. I wanted to see him desperately.

"Okay. Why don't you finish up from home today? Save you driving in the dark if you're tired."

The pondering took a nanosecond. I had promised my friend I would call at her house for a coffee on the way home and if I left early I'd definitely be in when Russ brought Edmund back—he was generally in the house when I got home as the nights were drawing in and Russ was cycling home. I did wonder why he was doing so much cycling—exercise I assumed.

"Yes, I'll do that. Would you be able to consolidate the Thompson data before I go, and erm, could you telephone Kieran and request we meet at my house at ten in the morning, rather than here?"

The extra time at home would guarantee I would be in when Russ collected Edmund too. Yes, I was becoming obsessed.

"Coffee?" my friend Alice asked.

I leaned back in the heavily cushioned chair in her orangery and crossed my legs.

"Erm, no thank you, honey. A glass of water would be great."

Alice gawped at me like I had just told her I was a post-op transsexual.

"Are you unwell? I thought water diluted the caffeine in your blood to a dangerous level," she remarked sarcastically. "Evian or sparkling Perrier?"

"Oh, it will be fine from the tap, thank you."

Alice scurried off as her remark and string of facial expressions hit home. My mood was indeed very strange. I generally drank eight pints of coffee during the day, only drinking water to break up the thirst. And I never drank tap water—it seemed wrong. She returned a few minutes later, handed me my tap water, complete with crushed ice and a slice of lemon, and took the comfy chair opposite.

"I've not seem you for ages. What have you been up to, Liv?"

I flicked a hand in the air. "You know. Just the usual. Work. Work. Work. Another boring dinner dance. Oh, and I erm, finally decided I've met the man."

I had no idea why I mentioned Russ; we weren't even going out and well, my friends. *Hmmm.* A big grin crossed her face and, although I knew I'd said too much, I wanted to gush.

"I thought you were glowing and I'm so glad you and Kieran got serious. He is so lovely and, given the reception he got with everybody at your sister's wedding, your family adore him as much as he does you."

I coughed into my water. "It's not Kieran. It's a guy I know called Russ."

"Oh. But, erm, poor Kieran. He's so nice. Erm, so where did you meet the new guy—through work?"

I shook my head. I was leading her down a very uncertain path. "In a bar. Well, that was the first place and then he got the gardener's job at the manor."

Her eyes grew and she tried very hard not to allow the concern/disapproval show on her face. "Gardener! What, is he shit rich and doing a manual job for fun?"

"No. I don't think he's rich at all. He's on the minimum wage and his shoes are dropping to bits," I admitted.

"Oh, my god!" Alice exclaimed, looking at me like I'd told her I was a post-op transsexual with a rodent shoved up my arse. "I hope you haven't slept with him—he'll be after your money."

Alice shook her head; I could not tell if she was horrified as to Russ' assumed and unproven dishonesty or disappointed as to my 'standards'. To her, poor and with scruffy shoes equated to dirty. And pre-Russ I, shamefully, probably would have thought the same.

"He's not interested in money and I have had sex with him," I returned.

Her hand flew to her open mouth.

"LIVIA," she screeched; "I think you're going fruit the loop. Gosh, how long have you known this guy?"

"A couple of weeks," I said nonchalantly, as the grin spread across my face. "But we erm, only kissed once and then we had sex last night."

"Where does he live?"

"I don't know."

"What about his family, friends? What does he do in his spare time—does he have interests outside of horticultural TV?" Alice teased.

I wished I'd never opened my mouth, not only because of the massive wall of prejudice, but because she was simply laying the harsh facts on the table. Yes. I knew nothing about the man I'd made have sex with me on the floor and, further to that, Kieran and I were complicated and everybody thought we were the perfect couple—which, on paper, we were.

"I've never met his family and I've only ever seen him with the guy he was with in the bar. And I don't have a clue about his interests. We don't talk all that often." God, it was sounding worse by the second. "And, erm, would you be as good as to not mention him when we are at Stones'—I'm not sure how Kieran will react."

Yes, we were having a nice little thirtieth birthday shindig in a few days and Kieran was my date.

An all-knowing smile appeared on her face. "Oh, I'm with you, Liv. You're up for a bit of bad boy before you and Kieran finally tie the knot. My lips are sealed. You can do promiscuity but you wouldn't let people down. As if you are going to get married to some broke gardener with scruffy shoes—your parents would go up the wall. I can see it now, your mother introducing Ester and Eddie—this is my daughter and her husband—he was educated at Oxford and owns a multi-national communications company. This is my other daughter Olivia and her husband—he owns a watering can and a spade."

She giggled. I did not.

"I'm sorry," Alice teased, rubbing my leg; "you have your bit of fun."

"I'm not having a bit of fun and I'm not having a fling before I marry Kieran. I think Russ might be the one."

Alice's features softened. "I think Kieran is the one; he can provide for you and he is lovely and successful. You're an analyst: a smart and pragmatic planner—you don't do things on a whim and you know Kieran can give you everything. What can this Russ guy offer?"

I looked away from Alice and to the apex of her garden room. At its point was a stunning stained-glass window through which the white light tumbled and was changed into something magical; it seemed symbolic. I wanted to say it; I wanted to tell her that Kieran, although brightening the edges, did not make me happy; I wanted to tell her that I was miserable and that I cried most days; I wanted to tell her that eating a peanut from a bowl on a bar would put me on the edge of a mental breakdown. But I said none of those things because weakness was not something to which I admitted.

I simply shrugged and said, "He offers what money cannot buy. He takes me for what I am. He accepts me for what I'm not. Would we still be friends if I suddenly said, Alice, I'm broke?"

"Yes. Of course we would!"

"Would you include me if I couldn't do retail therapy? Or expensive restaurants? Would you want to be seen with me if I wore scruffy jeans and an old coat?"

"Oh, Livia… now you're just being silly."

Alice smiled, though her eyes did not substantiate the gesture. Deep down she knew as well as I that, without our expensive shared interests, we would drift further apart until our association was a friendly hello when our paths crossed on the high street.

I changed the subject and drank my water because I wanted to go. I needed to get back to the manor.

To my disappointment, Edmund was curled up in his basket when I got home and, judging by the way he bounced off every inanimate object in sight when I walked in, he was either off his tits on amphetamines or had been inside all day. It appeared that Russ had not collected him and there were a few reasons as to why: he was sick or injured and hadn't turned into work, or he hadn't taken the dog because he didn't want to see me. I knew it was the latter and I didn't know what to do. Well, I knew the first thing to do: unless I wanted to be cleaning crap off my floor, I needed to take Edmund for a walk.

In the bedroom, I cast aside my pencil skirt, shirt and underwear, and then double socked my feet before heading off to find my wellies. Yes—I had naughtiness in mind.

The extended walk gave me chance to complete some seriously thorough reconnaissance. There was absolutely no sign of the groundskeeper anywhere. Not a trace. His hut was locked and his bike was missing though, through the window, I could see that his boots were absent from their usual spot and his trainers were left in their place. This ruled out illness or injury.

Suddenly, I was hurled back to the place where it was all utterly blank. I muttered a few miserable words to my innocent dog and veered to the dog area so he could have a run. I debated one myself but there was work to do and my stalking activities had not yet reached their conclusion.

It was dusk by the time I completed my list of reallocations for the Timpson account but, through the speckled-with-grey fading light, I could make out a single stream of smoke extending into the sky from the near distance. It emanated from the direction of the hut. I crossed my fingers and hoped Russ would be in his little sanctuary.

There was a nail-biting pause before the response to my tapping on the door and I wondered if he was considering pretending he was not there. The door swung open and I was greeted by a man looking much younger than the one I usually saw; Russ had taken the clippers to his face and taken several years off his projected age.

"Hi," I said, meekly.

"Hello."

He stepped away from the door, and quickly closed it after I passed through. And then there was an exchange of questioning looks but a restraint of words. He raised his eyebrows and, in doing so, invited the reason for my appearance.

I bit my lip. "I take it you're avoiding me?"

He took his seat back by the fire and gestured for me to sit opposite.

"I don't just do the garden, Livia—I av the estate to manage. I can't fix walls in a sheep field with a dog in tow—not unless you want him shooting." Russ paused and bit his lip too. "But yeah, I was avoiding you but now you're here I've changed my mind."

I tentatively offered my hand and, to my relief, he took it in his. "Why were you avoiding me?"

"I thought it'd be awkward and it's complex. You've 'ad your fun, Livia—just leave it, yeah."

I shook my head and looked around the small room with its old thick stone walls, a yellow-white Belfast sink in the corner, and a door I assumed opened into a toilet. There were rows of dilapidated shelves on one wall—the gloss paint yellowed and cracked and peeling up like flattened fingers in places. One side housed a bench which was covered by orderly piles of tools and pots of various sizes containing ironmongery of sorts. The whole room was illuminated by an unshaded bulb which cast the yellow glow of pre-energy efficiency and made everywhere look hazy. I was back in my dream and I relaxed into my chair and stared into the dancing, crackling flames of the fire.

"Do you want ta stay for a bit?"

I nodded. "Yes, if that's okay?"

"Yeah. But you'll 'av to let me work this order out. I've gotta phone it through in t' morning."

I smiled, inched my feet a little closer to the fire, and listened to the scribbling of the pen and the tapping of the buttons on the little red calculator. On finishing his scribing, Russ imparted a few inconsequential words. Smiling, I offered him my hand and he took it, interlinking his digits between mine. I closed my eyes and breathed in the blissful simplicity, and with every exhalation a little bit more of the nonsense of modern life left my heavy soul. And then he broke my reverie.

"Have you cried today, babe?"

"No. Not a single tear. You coloured me in with happiness last night, babe," I replied.

He laughed and, to my surprise, kissed the back of my hand. The butterflies in my tummy embarked on a riot.

"Colouring! Is that what you call it?"

It was my turn to laugh before I decided to pry.

"Why don't you talk, Russ? Are you always this quiet?"

He slowly shook his head. "Some people can't help but natter like my Mam and brother and some can't 'elp but be quiet like my Dad. I'm lucky enough to be able to choose. I'm happy with noise and I'm one of them lucky enough t' not be intimidated by silence. I'm quiet wi you for different reasons. It started cos I wanted to keep you away, but now I'm quiet cos you need me to be. Your busy, tormented mind needs some rest—you're on the edge, Livia."

I felt the tears build as the ball of difficulty rose in my throat.

"No crying, remember," Russ said to me, pitifully. "You're too susceptible to what's expected of you. Don't ever be like that wi' me cos I expect nothing—nothing at all."

I smiled and sat back in the chair. The flames were dancing and mesmerising and the crackling of the wood was audio bliss to my ears. No ringing phones. No tapping of computer keys. No static emanating from row after row of electrical devices. And I clung onto his hand and let myself be.

Sometime later, I became aware of the dying of the fire and the advancing time. He had a home to go to and I'd got a dog to feed.

"I better go, Russ. Sorry for keeping you. Please cycle home carefully. Perhaps you should start bringing the car now winter is about here?"

Russ sighed. "I can't—it's knackered. I was gonna fix it this month but I got me Mam a new washer instead. I'll sort it when I get paid."

"Oh."

The reality struck me. As a woman with two cars, I no longer considered a cycle as a mode of transport— it was exercise and recreation as far as I was concerned. Being without a car was incomprehensible too; when mine went for a service I got a courtesy car and I assumed people hired cars if without.

"Do you want the money? You can pay me back if it makes you feel better."

"Thanks, but no. I don't want your money."

"What about borrowing a car then?"

He gawked at me, incredulous. "The Porsche?"

"Oh no, I need that for work. My other car. I've got a Mitsubishi Evolution in my garage."

I didn't add that it was a car for which I'd paid tens of thousands of pounds and consequently drove just tens of miles. It was an impulse buy and a futile attempt at regaining a little of the carelessness of my youth; however, I bought the car, went out in it twice, and was so riddled with what if I crash, what will people think, and other assorted anxieties, the only time it went out after that was for its annual service whereupon I arranged for the dealer to collect it from home.

A childish grin crossed his face and I knew he was the boy who had found Willie Wonker's golden ticket. But the temptation was just that.

"Cheers, Livia. It's a nice thought but a car like that wouldn't last two minutes where I live. Come on." He stood up and straightened his cricked legs. "It's gettin' late."

I got up too and stretched my arms above my head. "I like it in here. Would you mind if I came again?"

"Nah. You've not been too much of a pain in the arse," he joked.

He would have earned himself a playful slap on the thigh if he hadn't intercepted the swing and caught my wrist. And that was it, the mood all changed and I no longer felt lethargic—I felt invigorated and very aroused.

"Guess what I'm wearing under this coat?" I provoked.

Russ looked me from head to toe, starting at my hair, running his eyes down my trendy, padded Rab trench-coat and stopping at my wellies.

"I don't know. Victoria's Secret. Versace suit. A ten-grand diamond necklace?"

I took a few steps closer and held out my hand. He took it and pulled me to him.

"Kiss me and I'll give you my diamond necklace," I flirted.

"I'm not interested in jewellery. Now scrapyard vouchers on the other hand…."

He stifled my laughter with a kiss and hummed in approval when he discovered I was, in fact, naked beneath my coat. I pushed him to the space before the dying fire, dropped to my knees, and used my embrace to force him to his too. And then he stopped kissing me, got to his feet, and hurried to the cupboard beneath the bench on the other side of the room. I was shocked and concerned; I thought he was rejecting me again before he returned with a long length of bubble-wrap which he laid on the stone floor and topped with a double thickness of fluffy horticultural cloche material. Following the construction of the ad-hock bed, he threw some more sticks on the fire and it started to burn as he came back to me on his knees.

"Now where were we, m' lady?"

"You were getting naked, Russel!"

He sniggered. "Oh yeah, I was."

Russ took a frustrating amount of time to explore my body with titillating touches and soft kisses that made me ache with yearning. My arms were wrapped around his neck and I was totally and utterly lost. Russ circled my thigh with his hand and pushed the leg to his waist. I wrapped it around him, along with the other one and then, consumed, I felt it build inside and I knew my orgasm was imminent. My climax crashed in time with his and we were melded together. Physically. Mentally.

Reality hit me at the same time as the soft kiss which landed on my head. Russ was real; we were real. The rest of it: the numbers on my bank statement, the messages on my phone, the social networking notifications—they were nothing more than distractions. But I was bored with distractions—the fleeting, unrewarding things which they were. I wanted Russ; he was everything that was something and nothing which was not. I knew he could make me happy and I wanted to make him happy too.

Chapter 10

Livia

Discreetly, I studied Kieran as he studied my summary. Dark roughened hair making him look CEO-from-a-dirty-novel hot. Well-cut shirt, the sleeves pinched closed by platinum cufflinks. Defined shoulders visible through the cotton. Muscular thighs pushing against his smooth, expensive trousers. Fresh aftershave breaking through the aroma of ground coffee.

Since my teens I'd had a list, mental of course, of the qualities I needed in the man with whom I would eventually settle down. Good looking. Wealthy. Educated. Solid background. Excellent career prospects. Oh, and the obligatory good sense of humour. I was looking right at my perfect man though something felt wrong. I ran my finger around the rim of my coffee mug as I mused. My list had changed and kind, generous, and understanding took pole position.

For fuck's sake.

Perhaps I was lost and then I'd been found.

Perhaps I was closer to meltdown than I thought.

Or perhaps it was because love, the indiscriminate, foolhardy thing that it was, had bombed into my life, bringing with it hurdles and strife and a world of confusion.

Clearly sensing my visual interrogation, Kieran raised an eyebrow and peered at me.

"I had planned on taking you to bed for an hour this morning but I need to get through this. I don't have time to do both," Kieran said. Flat. Business-like. Lacking in emotion.

"I'm not in the mood for sex, Kieran."

What I actually meant was that 'I'm not in the mood for having sex with you'; however, I thought the detail unnecessary.

"Well, I'm too busy for it anyway. And I'm not happy with this." He pointed at one of my investment proposals. "I suggest putting it in here—where I would get a decent return."

"No, Kieran, I would consider that short-sighted. I recommend you put it in the low risk investment as there is no early redemption penalty. Given the ebb and flow of your business there is a possibility you'll need to draw on the fund."

Kieran scratched the side of his head with his Parker pen.

"But it won't make much, Livia. Not much more than in a regular bank account."

"It will—have you seen the interest rates these days! Look, there'll be little gain, but if you channel it into a higher return investment and need to make a single withdrawal in the twelve-months you will actually lose money. Can you be sure you won't need to draw on the fund?"

I could see the wheels of consideration as they turned. Kieran owned a very successful business sourcing relatively small but specialist food producers across the world and establishing supply chains with small exclusive restaurant chains and niche food sellers. He identified the market gap just before the time that 'Fair Trade' and the whole ethical supply fashion took off and, through careful selection and my advice regarding shrewd investments, secured his wealth. He was good at his business but I was better at mine. I was an astute business analyst and knew that on several occasions during the last few years Kieran dropped upon an opportunity and needed to buy big and fast. Oddly for me, I chose not to fill the silence with justification and left it blank. Kieran had become greedy and short-term gratification often led to long term loss in my game; a game in which I excelled—half of my income being from commission and not salary. I wondered if Kieran had always been greedy and I'd failed to notice—just as I'd failed to notice his arrogance and snobbery before the night he confronted Russ.

"Fine," Kieran stated, as I turned around to see who was tapping at my French door.

I could not contain my delight as I skipped to the door and welcomed Russ inside—my welcome falling far shorter than Edmund's in the exuberance stakes—what with him bombing between my island and oak table like a wildcat liberated from a shoebox.

"All right, Ed," Russ muttered, looking thoroughly disheartened when he laid eyes on Kieran.

"I thought I'd pop in when I saw your car here. But erm, you've got company. I'll erm, see ya later."

"No, no. Please, come in—there's coffee in the pot. We're about done here."

Before he could refuse I was standing by the kitchen counter pouring a very large coffee that would take some time to drink. Russ reluctantly kicked off his work boots and took a seat opposite Kieran.

"Alright mate?" Russ asked.

Kieran raised a questioning eyebrow; he looked haughtier than I had ever known.

"Yes, fine." Kieran proffered a hand which Russ shook before returning to his slumped position. "I'm Kieran. Livia is my financial consultant."

Kieran did not apologise for his accusatory behaviour in the bar and by offering the initial greeting, in spite of Kieran's attitude, Russ had most definitely obtained the upper-hand. I noticed Russ' wry but slightly bitter grin as I placed his coffee in front of him, briefly touched his hand and retook my seat.

"It's not what she told me. She told me she was your client," Russ returned flatly—the enmity apparent as the two men, civilly, weighed each other up.

Two people could have not appeared so different. Kieran was sitting in his smart slate-grey trousers and slim-fit white shirt looking rakish, handsome, and totally composed; Russ slouched in the chair with his legs open, his hair looking like it had not seen a brush that day, let alone a styling product.

I intercepted diplomatically. "I advise Kieran and manage his financial affairs. This is Russ—as you know he's the groundskeeper here and I am his erm..."

I had no idea why I saw it necessary to complete the round of introductions and was stuck for words. What was I? I had previously said he was my friend but that seemed a little clinical given the recent events. Lover seemed excessive—we'd only had relations twice. And boyfriend—well that just seemed silly.

"She's become my pain in the arse," Russ interjected; "pinching my dog, turning up at my hut. Freeking cryin' on me at every opportunity."

I blushed deeply. Kieran had no idea that I was a mentally unstable, pill popping happiness fraud with an impressive collection of OCDs and a weeping habit; he only ever saw me polished, smiling and composed. He looked at me as if the claim incredulous. After a few minutes of rather tense but light-hearted conversational ping pong, my phone called out and bounced along the table. I caught it before it fell to the floor, saw it was my boss, and excused myself from the room.

Russ

"You'd be wise to disassociate your brain from your dick," Kieran said to me.

I glared at the man and ran through the possibilities: me failing to understand or him talking in Mandarin Chinese without me realising—and then I landed on the most likely option of him being a total cock.

"What?"

"It's pardon," Kieran said, like a condescending twat. "You. Livia. Just see it for what it is. Don't get involved."

"Thanks for the tip. What with me being a child an' you an adult I need all the help I can get," I replied, sarcastically.

"I'm a good ten years older than you and I'm offering advice because I know the bigger picture. I've seen men come and go—though hopefully you'll be the last. If you see Olivia as anything other than a good time, do one now. Save yourself the heartache of thinking you've landed the rich, beautiful woman, only to find yourself on the scrap heap and ruined for evermore."

I crossed my arms and slid a bit further down the seat. "Nah, p'raps you ought to do one seeing as you're her bloody escort. You're the one who takes money off 'er so don't look down your nose at me."

Kieran glanced at my work jeans—worn at the knee and so ingrained with dirt, nine weeks on a boil wash wouldn't get them clean.

"Ah, money. I thought it'd be about money looking at you." And then he did a fucking arrogant, conceited laugh. "Escort! Yes, I'm the escort who took her to Paris for five days in the spring—the escort who was on the top table at her sister's wedding—the escort who took her home and fucked her, for free, that time you saw us in town."

He did the rich twat laugh again and following the 'fucked her' comment I wanted to rip his head off.

"Russ," Kieran said, leaning across the table and dropping his voice; "quite frankly, I can't believe Olivia would be so indiscriminate or stupid enough to entertain somebody so close to home. I want you to walk away and find a girl from your neck of the woods. I don't want any trouble on her doorstep and be warned, when all is done, try your hand at stalking or harassment and you'll be sacked with a restraining order around your neck before you've drawn breath."

"And on that little threat, I better put my binoculars away and stop rummaging in her bin," I said, taking the piss. "Tell you what, Kieran, I'll manage my shit, you manage yours—"

"No, I'll tell you what," he interrupted, glaring; "I want you off the scene now. I don't like that she chose somebody who works a stone's throw from her house. I don't like that you turn up at her doorstep rather than meeting her at a hotel like the others did. I don't like those fucking looks she gives you..."

Oh, yeah. It turned out the smooth-enough-to-make-you-sick hero wasn't unflappable after all. His eyes were burning and his jaw tight.

"Perhaps those looks are because she likes me," I goaded.

"Or perhaps those looks are because she's going too fucking far— doesn't realise you're naïve and not one of the razor sharp usual brand. You are fucking deluded if you think Olivia is anything other than stoic."

"Stoic!"

"Yes, as in unemotional, unresponsive," Kieran snapped, assuming I didn't know the meaning of the word.

Yeah, he might have spent years looking at Liv but he never actually saw her: she was about as unresponsive as a colony of wasps whose nest had just been battered with a stick.

"I know what stoicism is—I got my education from my dad, not the shit comprehensive school I went to. And anyway. I don't think she's stoic, I think she—"

"I think she's what?" Livia strode into the room and dropped her glasses to the bridge of her nose.

"I think if she lost one more sandwich she'd be short of a picnic," I chided, only half joking.

"Well, luckily Waitrose do a great sandwich range and they deliver so the picnic shall be saved. I do hope you boys are getting along?"

"Like an 'ouse on fire," I replied; "but I better get my adoptive mutt and get on. We'll be out on t' estate today so don't panic if you get home early and we're not around. I've got a wall to rebuild before the next lot of sheep arrive. I might see you later, babe. You know where the hut is if you fancy a chill."

"Thank you, Russ."

I stood abruptly, whistled through my teeth, and Edmund appeared at my heels like greased lightning. "Come on Ed, we need to 'urry up. The delivery is being dropped up there and we've got to walk."

I tipped my chin at Kieran and winked at Livia. She took a few uncertain steps towards me, her hands hanging in the air, and then she dropped them and gave me a meek little smile. And I wanted to stride right over there and kiss her and pull her close. But I didn't. No. Because that's not how things were.

Chapter 11

Livia

After leaving Alice's house, I called Kieran and said that there was a change in the arrangements regarding dinner at The Stones restaurant and, as such, I did not need a date. He did not ask questions, probably on the assumption that it had changed from a couples to a girl's night, and so I happily spared him an explanation. I did not want to take Kieran; I didn't want to spend time with another man or want the awkwardness when I didn't want to sleep with him at the end of the night.

Following the cancelling of our arrangement, I tried to find Russ. After failing to locate my new favourite compatriot, I wrote a note and placed it on the top of his shoe in the hut. It politely asked Russ if he would like to be my date, told him the venue, and said, if he would like to come, to be at my house for seven. He left a reply on my table the following morning that said; 'Yes. See you later'. No elaboration. No kisses. No smiley faces. No unnecessary exclamation marks. No bullshit.

The evening arrived and Russ was due imminently. I was as nervous as hell and could feel the butterflies flapping in my tummy. The restaurant was quite exclusive and after trying on half of my wardrobe, I decided upon a dark red knee-length pencil skirt and a grey, fitted angora top. I finished my outfit with coordinating jewellery and some decent sized heels.

The meticulous attention to my appearance was most unusual when seeing my friends. When spending time with them I generally threw articles together— partly as an act of rebellion against the fact I needed to be so considered during the day and partly as I was the carefree, quirky one when we met and I liked to keep up that impression. In all honesty, it was my date I wanted to impress. I wanted him to like me, I wanted him to want me, and when I answered the door, he looked like he did.

I grinned like a Cheshire cat. Russ looked really nice in smart jeans and a blue polo shirt—the outfit only falling apart with the addition of a heavy coat and a woolly hat. In my naïve little mind, I assumed he would arrive by taxi under the premise of drinking. It hadn't crossed my mind he would come by push bike as his car was broken and he probably couldn't afford a taxi. As I welcomed him in I realised something I had never so much as considered: my head was up my arse and the world in which I circulated was not the one in which most people lived.

Russ warmly acknowledged the dog, took off his hat, and rubbed his head. His hair was fluffy, having recently been washed, and it stuck up at all angles following its liberation.

"Hot heels, Livia," he quipped. "And is my hat hair really bad?"

I nodded and reached to touch his hair before abruptly recoiling. I had no idea how to act without the social rituals which suddenly seemed to be pointless shenanigans. In my world, a date, Kieran for example, would place his hands on my forearms and plant a polite kiss on both cheeks as I pursed my lips and kissed the air. Why? I suddenly asked myself. I was English— not fucking French. I extended my hand, as was my new habit of crossing the boundary, and he took it in his and followed me to my bathroom.

"Do you really like my heels?"

Russ chuckled, "Yeah, they make your legs go on for miles an' if you wore em with stockings you'd look a right dirty cow."

Yes, I'd opted for the silk hold-ups.

"Do I look like the kind of girl who wears tights?"

Russ chuckled again. "Cheers, Liv. That's me hard."

We reached my bathroom whereupon I stood him by the mirror and rummaged in my hair cupboard for some kind of styling wax. I wore my hair shorter in the past and would rough it up and clip it when I wanted to look cool. Cool had not been in my description for a long time: I was safe and sensible. As I recalled, there was a blue tub with a silver lid labelled hair putty. I handed it to him and he removed the top and poked his finger inside.

"I'm more of a gel man myself..."

I watched him as he worked a bit of the wax between his fingers and started twisting and flattening. He turned to me with a questioning grimace.

I laughed and made an eek face back. Smart did not suit him.

"I haven't got any gel."

Russ turned on the tap, shoved his head into the flow of water, and rubbed off the lot before drying his hair using the towel which I passed him.

"Oh fuck it," he muttered; "I'll leave the hat off—it'll be alright by the time we get there."

He followed me out of my bathroom and, without forethought, I turned abruptly and stopped by the bed.

"Russ, I don't know what to do."

"About what?"

I flicked my hand between us.

"Ha ha. You don't know what to do cos I'm not a trained monkey—and that's what your used to dealing wi'. And I'm playing it cool as I don't do all that 'ha, ha, har' bullshit and I'm scared if I do what I want to do you'll run a mile. By the way, I'm twenty-six, how old are you?"

"Erm, thirty-one."

"Even better. The disapproval only builds," he teased. "Your friends are gonna think you've lost the plot when you turn up with me."

I knew just what he meant. I was the successful, rich woman who dragged a handsome businessman around and drove a Porsche; he was the working-class, younger man—the total opposite to my usual type. Everybody would think I was having a premature midlife crisis and opting for a bit of uncut diamond.

I chewed my lip. "And what to you want to do that'll scare me away?"

He smiled the one-sided, naughty smile I daydreamed about.

"Check out those stockin's and fuck you silly on that bed."

He tipped his head towards my silk sheets and blushed. I knew he regretted his bluntness but I loved it. No talk of wining, dining, or making love.

"Let's make a deal," he proposed. "Abandon the expectations and follow our feelings, yeah?"

He held out his hand and I shook it, wondering what I was agreeing to. I didn't have any complaints at the first act: that which involved me being thrown onto my back with my skirt around my waist and his head between my legs within thirty-seconds. And then I made it all a bit strange when he tried to kiss me on the lips.

"I'm sorry. I erm, can't." I pushed on his chest and moved my face away from his.

I sat up and put my hands on the bed behind as he knelt between my legs.

I was at it again: I was about to spew another one of my strange ideas and if he stuck around for much longer I would wonder who was the weirdest. First, I admitted my obsession with hand hygiene and eating, and then my even number OCD, and now I'd brought up my issue of kissing anybody after their mouth had touched me intimately. I did not need to; nobody else had ever guessed because I was the master of avoidance.

"Babe, if it's the taste you're worried about, don't—you taste amazing."

I'd totally ruined the moment but, whereas he seemed subdued, that comment made me even hornier. *He liked it.* If he was only doing it to pleasure me he would not have said that.

"I don't know—it's not just the taste—it's the thought. I've got this thing and kissing after, erm. I don't know," I rabbited like a soul deranged; "it's just too much to deal with."

On that, he pinned me with those searching, intense eyes of his and very deliberately put his middle finger in his mouth. Yes. I was getting even hornier in spite of him challenging me with more confrontational therapy. And then he pulled his middle finger from his mouth and held his first finger out to me. Oh, it appeared there had been two fingers and a mouth involved down there. My heart thumped a bit harder at the thought of putting that finger in my mouth.

"Babe, you have no idea what watching you suck that finger will do for me," he said, with a very naughty grin.

I shook my head to decline and he offered the middle one, the one that had already been in his mouth, and the whole issue of my body fluids was diluted somewhat. I started to make justifications—the finger was in me but then it went in his mouth and his mouth was on me....and then I stopped my mental ramblings and put his thick digit in my mouth.

And it wasn't bad.

His scintillating eyes drove me to pull his hand away and put the un-licked finger in my mouth too. It was not how I thought—amazing would not have been my chosen adjective but how I tasted was definitely not offensive.

Russ looked on with wanting and passion but above all patience. Everybody else wanted something but he was happy to let me be. And I wanted him to be happy. I wanted to please him and, at that moment, I would have done anything to do it. Those neuro-chemicals were mashing with my mind again and taking their healing eraser to soften the dark lines of my anxieties.

"Please could you try to kiss me?" I whispered, already cringing at the thought.

"I'd love to. You ever kissed anybody before?" His voice was low, scratchy, and it hit me straight between the legs.

I smiled. "There was this one guy—in a toilet, in a bar. Have you ever kissed anybody before?"

"There was this one girl—in a toilet, in a bar…"

The first kisses were barely there and with a closed mouth as he tested my response. I was reserved, I was apprehensive, but I soon realised that it was another thing I had built into a monster. I didn't even panic when his tongue touched mine. No. I grabbed his hair, laid back on the bed, and pulled him down with me.

I didn't admit any crazy mental obsessions during act two, though he never got to 'fuck me silly on that bed': I shoved him on his back and 'fucked him silly' instead. I took a brief laughter break halfway through when he asked me to say, 'I'm going to fuck you silly', as apparently, me saying rude things 'is really fucking hot' with my 'posh voice'. It was over a decade since I had laughed during a session and it made me love the whole thing even more.

Thirty-minutes later, I'd replaced my laddered stockings with another pair, his hair was looking even worse than when he first removed his hat, and we were late. The taxi waiting outside sounded its horn and I was going to be introducing my now, yes, official lover to my friends still wearing a post-orgasmic glow.

Not that I cared.

I didn't care what they thought of me or if they would like him. I simply wanted to keep the wonderful feeling that came with him in my life.

Chapter 12

Russ

I told my Mam I was going out for tea with a girl I met at work. I tried to sound all casual and play it down but I knew my rabbiting and then brooding gave my nerves away. Livia was not a girl, she was an enchantress, and the place we were going was in constant battle for Michelin stars. After checking out the place on the net, I knew the shirt I'd borrowed from my brother and my best trainers were going to look out of place but I didn't have any choice. I considered wearing my leather 'interview, wedding and funeral' shoes but they would look stupid with jeans and I would have looked like a waiter in my black trousers.

Yeah, I was shitting myself—not because I cared what people thought of me but because I didn't want people to think bad of her. Livia was a box of eggs on a Motocross bike and, for all I knew, a surprised expression or a disapproving stare from her beloved posh mates might send her to the nearest corner to rock, cry, and count shit for ever more. And I was really scared of her losing it—really fucking scared. Yeah, Kieran might be a shallow knob but at least he was safe—whereas me on the other hand…

Livia looked amazing. I couldn't believe she asked me to be her date: not when she had that Kieran bloke hanging on her every word. I reckoned he was in love with her and, reading between the lines, he wasn't happy about me and thought if he was on her scene long enough he'd be the one. I suspected he was right—after all, he'd been around for years and I'd been around for weeks.

There were only eight tables in the whole place—round ones with stiff white tablecloths, real orchids, and cutlery polished so much you could make it into a telescope and look at the freekin' moon.

Yeah, I was nervous.

Sickeningly out of my depth nervous.

Livia towed me into the room and spotted her friends before the waitress got to us to show us to our seats. There were another three couples already at the table, sipping wine and chatting politely. I noticed their surprise when they saw me and a few of the women barely managed to stop their jaws from dropping when they saw Livia holding my hand. Gripping it with one hand or circling it with two—it had fast become a habit and I'd started searching her out without thought too. I was totally confused—in at the deep-end confused.

"Evening all," Livia swooned.

I pulled out her chair. Yes. I didn't do the fake hugging or the air kissing but I had been brought up with good manners. I always said please and thank you, opened doors, and gave my seat on the bus to pregnant women and little old ladies.

"Hello." I cringed. All eyes were on me. Every bloody eye. They weren't expecting me. They were expecting Kieran.

As the waitress handed us two Hessian-backed, tall, thin menus, Livia made the introductions. The girl sitting on my other side was Sophia—a little, dark-haired woman who on first impressions appeared stuck up. Her husband, Conner, was beside her. Then there was Ellie, who I met a few days earlier, and her 'partner' Alistair. He was beside Alice, who took the seat next to her husband, James.

"This is Russ," Livia stated.

There was no description of our relationship—though what could she say—it was the first time we had been out together, we'd only been intimate for a few days, and we never talked about what we were doing. There wasn't really any point—we wouldn't be doing it for long.

I said hello again and turned my attention to the menu, flinching when Livia's hand landed on my thigh. I felt like the local tramp at a royal wedding. I scanned the pages; there were mussels, pate, and other stuff that sounded grim to start, and trout, duck, sea bass, roasted butternut squash for main. My eyes went up and down but my peripheral vision still clocked Sophia rudely mouthing something to Livia across me. 'Where is Kieran?' I didn't see Livia's reply though I saw the flush spread across her face when I turned and asked what she wanted to eat.

"So then," the woman, Sophia, directed at me, "who are you Russ—when and where did you come from?"

I was unsure at what to say before I settled on the truth. "I'm a nobody; the groundskeeper at Livia's house. I only really came on the scene when I dragged that mangy mutt of hers out of the lake. I've tried and failed to avoid her ever since."

I tipped my head towards Livia and she huffed, elbowing me in the ribs.

"We share custody of Edmund now," Livia intercepted. "Yes, I actually trust somebody with my dog!"

"Oh my gosh," Sophia exclaimed, "you've never even trusted me with him and we've been friends for years."

"Yeah, there's a reason for that. He'd come back smelling like he'd been to a tart's parlour. Sophia is a beauty therapist," Livia informed me.

She was not the kind of girl I'd met doing a Beauty Therapy NVQ at the tech—good at nail extensions and eyebrow plucking.

"Sweet. Where do you work?" I asked.

"Oh, I own my own studio. I have another two ladies working for me," Sophia scoffed.

"Yes, and she does a mean facial," Ellie quipped.

"I'll bear that in mind," I replied flatly.

"It might be 'mean' but it costs the earth. How do you justify a hundred and twenty pounds to have your face washed, Sophia?" Alistair teased.

Sophia glared at the big bloke sitting opposite. "It's not face washing! Exclusive products and non-surgical facelifts come at a price."

I held out my hands and turned them over and over. "Have you got any idea how I can get the muck out of these?"

I showed her my palms before curling my fingers so she could see the tips. They were permanently engrained with dirt. I scrubbed my hands, I really did, but it never came out, even after a soak in the bath. Sophia tried to disguise her look of disgust and hovered her hands over mine—she didn't touch them. Livia, on the other hand, grabbed me.

"Your skin's dry, Russ. So it traps the dirt. I'll give you some hand cream but don't worry about it. I think your hands are kinda hot. Don't be embarrassed about working for a living," She studied my fingers like they were something special. "Oh look, this one bears the image of Christ."

Livia kissed the fingertip under scrutiny and I could not believe she, with her crazy if illogical cleanliness OCDs, kissed the ingrained dirt on my finger.

I was surprised and very confused.

The woman was as clear as mud.

After recent events, I'd decided she probably wanted me for a bit of novelty sex, but that wasn't sexual: it was affectionate—as was the hand holding. I reckoned, given their silence and questioning expressions, everybody else at that table was surprised too—not that I cared. The recollection of Kieran's bitter comment about Livia 'going too far', on the other hand, really fucking stung...

"Take it by the look on their faces you never kissed Kieran's finger at the table?" I teased.

"No."

"And she never held his hand." Alice nodded at our woven fingers. "Keep a tight grip, Russ—you'll need it with her."

I expected a joke or a smart-ass return, but the look Livia gave me said it all: she wasn't thinking of running. I, on the flip side, was wondering how much I could push the deal I'd made with myself to only see her while ever we could walk away reasonably unaffected. The deal started at one kiss, then one time for real, then one date, and right then I was thinking one more week. The thing about us both been unaffected was totally trashed: I was already walking away from her as a collection of mangled thoughts and jaded body parts.

"And back to kissing," Ellie butted in; "we never saw her kiss Kieran at all!"

Ellie followed the comment with a wink, not that I saw the end of it. Livia, the rampant woman, grabbed my jaw and stuck her face to mine. Tongues and all. At first, I thought she was making a point but a few seconds in I changed my mind. She was well into the kiss and so was I. Her hands touched my face, she set a soft, slow pace and her breaths quickened—as did mine. She was becoming a drug. I was dragged from my dream by a deliberate cough and the grating voice of the woman sitting on my left.

"Oh for god sake. Somebody make it stop."

I did: I made it stop for fear of losing my mind. Livia was flushed and her eyes were glazed and I could read that mind of hers. Yeah. Perhaps she wanted me for sex after all.

A woman in a black skirt and white blouse appeared, nodded at the open bottles of red and white wine, and asked me and Livia what we would like to drink. Livia requested red and, what with me being indifferent, I said red like her. The waitress began taking the food orders, scribbling in her pad as she went. As she went around the table I started to fret. Arse. I think Livia sensed my panic and leaned her alluring self closer to me.

"Fancy having the same as me, babe? It's always better to match on garlic, oh, and by the way, I'm paying tonight, it's my friend's birthday. You can pay next week."

Next week? If she meant it that was one week out of the window—I hoped she liked the chippie. She said the last comment loud enough for the others to hear and I knew she was trying to ease my worry. Yes, I'd scanned the menu and nearly pulled a sickie when I saw the prices. Twenty-eight quid for a plate of food—the world was officially radio rental! I shrugged, nodded, and told her to choose away. She chose seared duck with cherry sauce for the starter, fillet steak for the main, and told me to pick the pudding later.

As we waited for the first course the talking bounced around the table. Nothing challenging and nothing controversial but, in spite of Livia and especially her friend Ellie and her fella trying to include me, I felt like the black sheep. It turned out the next lowest person after me in the job pecking order was Alistair and he was a structural engineer with his own building firm. Her other two girl-friends were lawyers, one of the husbands was a divisional HR manager (whatever the hell that was), and the other husband owned a chain of gyms. He struck up a conversation asking if I worked out and I told him I did weights twice a week with my brother—the rest of my physique being down to good genes and manual labour. He asked me where I trained and rapidly changed the subject when I told him. Alistair, the big bloke, seemed quite down to earth and diverted the subject by saying that good old-fashioned sport was better than the gym. He asked me if I played football, cricket, rugby, basketball, or water polo.

"Take it you like ball games?"

"God yeah. I'd have been hanging off a bridge if it wasn't for my ball games quite a few times over the last few years," Alistair told me.

His girlfriend elbowed him in the ribs. "You'll be hanging by your balls if I have to spend another night with wall-to-wall Sky Sports."

Alistair smiled. "Looks like I'm up for a grim crucifixion then."

I was telling him how I had started playing pub league football when the food arrived. I say food. It was more like art. And, although the portion was small enough to feed Tinkerbell, it was good. Really bloody nice. It was cooked on the edges and pink in the middle and the sauce was a million times nicer than the stuff you had on your ice cream when you were a kid.

Just as the last of the group cleared their plates, my phone buzzed in my pocket; I'd turned the ring off but I needed to see who it was. My mates could wait but if it was my Mam in a major mess or brother back in trouble, I'd leave without seeing the main course or pudding. I excused myself, pulled the phone from my pocket, and looked at the missed call.

"I'm really sorry. Could you excuse me. I need to return this call. It's me Mam."

I took the napkin off my lap and placed it on the table before I went outside.

Livia

"What?" I snapped at Sophia, her judgemental eyes on me as soon as Russ left the room.

"Err. Liv. Are you having some kind of breakdown? Dumping Kieran to shag your gardener. I know he's young but you are not old enough to need a toy-boy. Kieran is lovely and rich and absolutely dotes on you. And he just left the table to make a call halfway through dinner. How rude," Sophia scoffed.

"She hasn't dumped Kieran," Alice interrupted, "so don't mention this guy to Kieran when you next see him. And anyway, Liv, I thought Kieran was coming tonight—did something come up?"

"Yes. I left yours, phoned him, and said it wasn't appropriate for him to accompany me. I haven't dumped Kieran because we were never together and I'm not just shagging my gardener. Jesus, Sophia—how shallow do you think I am?" I slapped my head at the final comment. "Okay, I take that back. My past words and actions have at times qualified as such."

I was shamefully the woman who had come out with classic comments such as 'Sex is a biological function—I only do it because I like getting fucked'. I had probably rightfully earned the label 'shallow'.

"And anyway," I continued, "I think it's nice he prioritises his mother over the opinions of people he just met. Where do your parents come in your pile of priorities, Soph? I know mine disgracefully don't even qualify on a day-to-day basis."

"The gym he goes to is as rough as hell. And it's renowned for drugs," Conner added, meekly. "He seems a nice enough lad but you don't want to get involved with people who do drugs."

"Lad!" My so-called friends were ripping in as soon as he left the room and I was enraged.

"I hate to state the obvious, Livia, but he's quite a bit younger than you," Alice chipped in.

I shook my head at the extent of their disapproval.

"Oh, fuck off—the lot of you," I snapped. "If I brought a man five years my senior you wouldn't bat an eyelid."

"I would if he turned up here dressed like some student going to the happy hour at the local Weatherspoon's," replied Alice. "He should have at least put a pair of trousers on. What the hell is the matter with you? I can't believe he is the man you were gushing about at mine—at very least I expected somebody with, with…."

"With what?" I pressed.

James finished her sentence with 'prospects'. I was shocked and horrified and I was ashamed of them—not Russ.

"Steroids are bad news," James added. "And they can make people aggressive."

"Who says Russ does drugs?" I spat.

Conner shrugged, "He's a big bloke to be only working out twice a week."

"He builds walls and digs holes for a living!"

"Hey, I'm a big bloke and I never set foot in a gym and I don't take drugs," Alistair added, in Russ' defence.

"Yes Alistair but, no offence to him, you don't look like you could have walked off a council estate," Sophia said. "If the world was different and Livia introduced you to her parents as her future husband they would be happy for her. If she took him, in his trainers," she sneered, "they would be gutted."

"Why?"

"Livia," said Ellie softly, "calm down—what Alice means is that, as nice as he seems, at our age we have to think about settling down with somebody who will provide for us when we have children. That's all—don't take it personally."

I pressed my teeth together. I was a second away from causing a massive scene when a hand curled around my shoulder.

"Everything alright, babe?" I asked Russ—my sarcastic name-calling sticking as a term of endearment.

"Yeah. It's just me Mam. She gets 'erself in such a state sometimes. They got burgled five years back and it right shook her up. We keep tellin' her it won't happen again, but when none of us are about…" He seemed to drift into thought. "Anyway, she's fine. I phoned Mrs Crosby next door and she's poppin' round and making her a cuppa."

"Have you installed an alarm? That might reassure her," I said.

Russ shook his head. "No. It won't 'appen again."

"You sound very certain," Alice said; "did the police actually catch the people who did it?"

"No, me and my brother did. Anyway, have I missed owt?"

"Conner was just saying how your gym has a drug problem. Do you take steroids?"

I didn't feel the need to ask but I wanted my friends to see his reaction. Not flinching, Russ continued topping up our wine glasses.

"No I don't, and his gyms 'll have a drug problem too."

Conner did flinch; he sat up in his chair and dropped his forearms heavily on the table—clearly irate following the perceived slur on his high-end leisure facilities. "They're not 'gyms', they are health clubs and you won't find drug users in my establishments."

"Steroids are everywhere," Russ said. "The modern obsession with physical appearance is not class specific—though the naive assumption as to how people achieve their goals probably is. I assume the upper classes look like they do cos of personal trainers, liposuction and Botox. The upper classes assume the likes of me look like this cos of illegal drugs and mindless heavy-weight bench-pressing."

Bang.

There was silence.

I grinned and slapped my palms on the table. "And that is just one of the reasons I will love this man."

I could not believe what I had just said—nor could my open-mouthed friends or Russ— judging by the choking and the wine coming down his nose. And I could not believe the extent of my dishonesty either—I was not going to love him because I loved him already. I probably always would. It was as clear as day.

"The ice queen has finally melted," Ellie exclaimed excitedly; "and what are the other reasons?"

"I'm hung like a donkey," contributed a partially recovered and grinning Russ.

I placed my hand on his and decided to go on seeing as I'd started.

"Yes. The large penis is a bonus," I said; "but more impressive is his effrontery—challenging without dancing around and giving a shit what you think. But something I love as much as his words are his lack of them. Most of us in the shitty modern world never properly listen—we hear and then we respond, and we keep going even when we are wrong. He hasn't got that disease. We just talk and talk and fucking talk and it all becomes noise."

"I'd describe it as a tumult," Russ interjected flatly, totally taking the piss.

I leaned past my quite shell-shocked date and glared at Sophia. "And while we're clearing things up; yes, Kieran is lovely, good to look at and he's not bad in bed. He says the right things, he's loaded, behaves correctly, and would never raise the subject of his penis here at the dinner table, but that's because he's a trained monkey. If you like Kieran so much bloody have him, Sophia—he charges four-hundred quid for an average night but he'll give you mate's rates if I ask him."

I snatched my wine glass from the table and downed the lot. And I wasn't just angry, I was horny too. Russ put a not so gentle hand around the side of my head, pulled me towards him and kissed me on the temple.

"You could have squashed that rant into two sentences," he said, flatly.

Yes, I loved the man already.

I needed to go pee and so I excused myself and headed for the bathroom.

Sitting on the toilet, I tried to clarify my thoughts. I had fallen irrationally fast and scarily deep for somebody who was so far removed from my usual choice in men it was unreal. And Russ was right about many things; my boyfriends since uni were all, to a greater or lesser extent, trained monkeys, which led to the sobering thought that I was the biggest trained monkey of them all; I was susceptible to what was expected of me and I adopted those expectations as my ideals—safe circle of friends, high earner, successful career, exclusive house, Porsche, designer clothes, personal trainer—from the outside looking in I had it all but I seriously wondered if it was what I wanted.

I reluctantly dragged myself from the peace and quiet of that cubicle, washed my hands, and opened the door leading to the corridor.

"Bloody hell, Livia," Russ exclaimed, clutching his chest.

Yes, I did fling the door open a little exuberantly.

"Sorry I made you jump."

"Livia—do you really pay that bloke four-hundred quid to go out with you?"

I nodded and made an eek face.

"Christ—you've got more money than sense!"

I smiled. "I suppose I have. But I've got a massive amount of money and so I won't take that accusation offensively."

Russ chuckled. "Liked your little rant out there. Not sure what your friends are saying now though."

"Oh fuck 'em."

I grabbed his shirt and dragged him into the ladies' washroom.

"What the hell are you doing, Liv?"

I pushed him into the cubicle, jostled for position, and locked the door with a piece of toilet paper.

"Oh," he said with a wry grin, slid his hands under my jumper and kissed me.

I could not believe I was in a toilet cubicle with a man while my friends waited at the table. I grabbed him through the fabric of his pants and his roving hand travelled up my skirt. With brazen abandon, I snatched off my knickers, and crammed them into his back pocket.

"Liv. Livia. Stop," he whispered, prizing his mouth from mine. "We're in a toilet and anybody could come in and we used the last jonnie before we came out."

"Have you always practised safe sex?" I asked bluntly.

"Yeah."

"Well, I've never had unprotected sex either."

I saw the wheels turn in his head. I knew he was tempted and I knew he was excited; I still had my hand around him and he felt fit to burst.

"Bloody hell, Liv. You're such a bad influence. You're gonna get me in shit, I swear."

Russ circled my thighs with his hands and pinned me against the wall. Almost immediately, however, he stilled me with his frame and, biting his lip and looking to the ceiling, held me totally still.

"Oh shit," he cursed; "you feel amazing."

I dared not breathe until I knew the danger was past and when he started to move I'd totally lost the ability. Things had quickly become how I'd never imagined: slow, deliberate, and totally awe inspiring.

Within seconds I was close and then the washroom door opened, a cubicle door locked, and the sound of a woman peeing bounced around the room. Russ put his hand over my mouth and the humour crossed his eyes as I bit down to stifle my groans. I couldn't believe he managed to hold on until the water stopped running, the hand drier stopped blowing, and the little automatic squirt of air freshener signified the visitor had left the room. And then it was just us and we finished what we had started. I opened my eyes to find him looking straight back at me, the corners of his mouth upturned in a restrained smile; he stroked his lips across mine and kissed the corner of the unrestrained grin I returned. I was falling: hopelessly, madly falling into some place I'd never been.

"I take it you're on the pill," he asked, as we furtively emerged into the corridor.

"Not exactly," I replied; "never needed it. Always used condoms. I'll get the morning after pill. And the pill."

Russ said my actions were irresponsible and I considered myself suitably reprimanded. We retook our seats and Russ chose us the dark chocolate torte. Not that I was thinking about dessert. I wanted to take him into my bed. Cuddle him all night. Wake up with him in the morning. Just be with him. Final.

Chapter 13

Russ

I couldn't see where I was going in that puddle of mud; all I knew was that things were going to end badly. I needed the no nonsense, black and white insight of my father but I couldn't talk to him about Livia—not unless I wanted a two-hour lecture before he kicked me out on my arse. Cos the thing with discrimination is the largely ignored reality that usually it's two-way traffic.

I looked at her peaceful sleeping face, her cheek pushing up to a ball where it rested on the pillow. The silk bloody pillow. I couldn't believe I was in a bed with white silk sheets with a beautiful, smart, passionate woman, and have the urge to sneak out and run fast and far. Not that I could. I didn't have it in me to leave her and that's why I knew I ought to. The longer I stuck with her the more people would get hurt and I didn't want to hurt anybody.

The night before confirmed what I already knew: I could ignore what they thought of me but I couldn't ignore what I thought about them—or what they thought about Livia for associating with somebody like me. With Livia, I didn't have to try but with some of her friends I fought to hide the resentment inside me: the resentment towards the higher classes which was planted by my father and nurtured by my circumstances. I didn't resent them because of what they'd got: I resented them for judging me because of what I hadn't. All they saw was my lack of possessions but, in turn, I saw their lack of solidity. I was certain you could take away my unpolished outer shell and find rock-hard loyalty, bollocks and principle inside—and I thought that was more valuable than flashy clothes or a shit-hot career. The likes of Livia's friends crossed the street to avoid the bloke sitting on the pavement with a scruffy dog whereas I crossed it to give him fifty pence or buy him a cuppa—not because I was a hero, but cos I treated others as I'd like them to treat me. End of.

I changed the subject on purpose when I mentioned the burglary. It wouldn't happen again because nobody on the outside would bother to pilfer our houses and nobody on the inside would dare with me and Zac on the scene. I'm glad Livia didn't push the subject or ask questions. My head was in the clouds and I couldn't stand the thought of it crashing down. It would come down eventually but I wanted to be with her as long as I could. How long I didn't know. Yeah—I'd lost my mind—I was officially madder than a bloke with a lifelong exposure to heavy metals. It was easier when I thought she was just using me for sex but, at the restaurant, she said love and I didn't want to hurt her.

Her bleary eye opened. "Hi."

"Mornin." I pushed a long bit of her dark fringe off her face. "Your hair is mental."

In the day when, it was brushed and styled, her hair was a long choppy bob thing but, right then, it looked like a bush. I twisted a lock around my finger.

"How do you decide where to put this bit? It's poking forward but it seems like it should go back." I pulled at another section. "Bloody hell, Livia, your hair is wicked. You went to sleep looking like Grace Kelly and woke up looking like Worzel Gummidge."

"Sorry, it's always like this until I've been in the shower and attacked it with the straighteners."

I buried my fingers in her mop and made it even worse.

"Nah, leave it. It makes you look feral—though after last night I think you are feral. I can't believe you made me shag you in a toilet. Have you got some public convenience fetish or summot?"

A cute red flush spread across her cheeks and attempted to get down her neck. "No, cheeky. I never did it in a toilet. I never did it anywhere public at all. It's you. You make me naughty."

"Yeah, very. You are going to the chemist's today, aren't you?"

We'd had unprotected sex three times and if she was going to get all 'no it'll be fine' on me there was a good chance I was in deeper shit than I could handle.

Livia nodded. "Yes."

"Good." I gave her a quick kiss and jumped out of bed.

Livia's face dropped. "I hoped you could hang around—what with it being Saturday. Are you doing a runner?"

"No. I thought I'd put the kettle on if you don't mind me in the kitchen. I won't find your cupboards filled with maids, cleaners, and male sex-workers, will I?" I joked. Not that I found it funny that she hired Kieran to shag her—not that his version of the story matched hers but he was obviously bitter and she had no reason to lie...

Livia shook her head and smiled and I stomped naked into the kitchen to make the tea and feed the dog.

Livia

I hotfooted to the en suite to pee, clean my teeth, and have a quick shower before Russ got back. I'd lived in my house for a long time and nobody had slept in my bed. I always kicked Kieran out post-coitus and my previous boyfriend didn't even make it through the front door—it was always his house or a hotel— enough said. Russ, however, I wanted to keep there forever and it scared me. I padded back into the bedroom, clad in a fluffy white towel, just as my mobile phone started to ring. I dropped my bottom onto the bed, huffed, and picked up the phone just as a single kiss landed between my bare shoulder blades. Then another. Then another. Oh, gosh, I was close to gasping.

"Good morning." It was my boss.

I knew what was coming before it even arrived. There was an issue with a big client, the values of their shares were falling, and they wanted to pull out and get things reorganised for the start of play on Monday. My boss had arranged for them to go to the office at eleven where both he and I would meet them to discuss the plan. *You have got to be joking me.* I bit my tongue and did the performing chimp dance which I did so well.

"Yes. I'll get sorted and be there."

I ended the call and my shoulders rounded as my head dropped. I did not want to talk money and investments and spend my Saturday morning securing the privilege of some already very privileged individuals. I wanted to stay with Russ, loll about in my pyjamas with 'mental hair' and be human: a real, living, breathing entity. His knees drew either side of my hips and his bristly chin scratched against my neck.

"What's up, babe?" he asked.

And that was it, the ball of disappointment which was stuck in my throat shape-shifted into water and, yet again, I was weeping like an irrational, pathetic fool.

"Hey, hey. What's 'appened?" Russ grabbed my knees and turned me towards him.

He studied my face as he stroked my hair and I was glad when he pulled me onto his chest—I didn't want him to see my weakness yet again.

"I've got to go to the office."

It sounded even more pathetic when I said it out loud. I was sobbing like a child because I needed to get dressed, put on some make-up, get in my Porsche, drive to an ivory tower, and chew the cud for an hour or two.

"I'm sorry. I'm being silly. There are people in this world who are homeless, starving, and dying in wars and I'm crying over this. I'm ridiculous."

"Just phone him back and say no," Russ said, as a matter of fact.

It all seemed so certain coming from him. Black and white; pure and simple. But it wasn't.

"I can't. I have to go. It's my job. I can't risk losing my job."

"Why?"

"Because I need the money," I replied, amazed by his rudimentary question.

He rubbed his gravelly palms up and down the tops of my arms and made me look at him. He couldn't help but cheer me up without imparting a single word. The half-beard was back, his hair was in disarray and he was sitting, shamelessly naked, without a care in the world.

"Babe, you don't need much money at all. It's a trick by the bad men in the establishment. They teach us we need so much money to tame us—then they can cream off their profits. They drive us down and keep us needy so all that's left is to separate us. Cubicles in offices. Isles in supermarkets. It's not organisation—it's not progress—it's dividing and conquering. A lot of money is something you want. Not something you need."

I turned my palms upwards. "Russ, this house is paid for but the ground rent is as much as a mortgage on your average two-bedroom terrace. My utility bills are a fortune; I spend hundreds of pounds a month on fuel. My outgoings are fucking massive. I cannot rock the boat because I can't afford to lose my job. It's different for you."

"We both need to eat, drink, and be dry and warm. You share my sky— we can't be that different. Look how bloody miserable you are, Liv? I don't cry and even if I did a Porsche wouldn't stop me crying. Laughing with my mates would. Sitting around a table with my Mam, Dad and brother would. Watching your stupid dog get his face stuck in a rabbit-hole would. Makin' love to you would," he said, with a wink. "Babe, you're spendin' your life without renewing it. How often do you see your friends? Your folks? When was the last time you took a walk without watching the clock? When was the last time you enjoyed being alive?"

He was right. He was right but I had that irritating modern disease and I had to return a noise.

"I don't have time."

Yes, it was a pitiful return and I doubted I could ever be cured.

"Make time. You must be good at what you do, Liv—if they appreciate you they'll appreciate you regardless. If they don't, fuck 'em. Find something else."

"It's not that easy," I returned. "Have you got any idea how much I earn with them, Russ? I brought home about ten-grand a month last year. I earn that money because of what I've built up and I need it now."

"Babe. Ditch the personal trainer and spend that three hours running 'round the fields with Ed or riding your bike. Sack the cleaner and buy a pair of rubber gloves. In fact, a bit of muck would do you good. Stop working so late every night and you can abandon the nine gallons of coffee every day and the Waitrose ready-meals and eat some cheap, decent snap. And as for paying Kieran to take you out and shag you—don't even get me started on that."

"I've got a therapist too," I muttered.

"You don't need a therapist, Liv. You need a break."

"I do need a therapist. I'm mental."

"You're not mental. You've got a few OCDs but they aren't the end of the world. Random, yeah. Destructive, no. If they were destructive, the food on dirty fingers would run into not eating out in case people had touched the food without you knowing and—"

I stopped him with a look. I didn't want any more paranoia to deal with. I opened my mouth to respond and he silenced me with a kiss. A very brief kiss before he grabbed my hand and pulled me off the bed, the towel making a hasty retreat and leaving me as good as naked as he marched me into the living room. He walked determinedly around, flicking at switches: the internet modem, my computer (which was always on standby), the smart TV, and the timer that turned on my lamps. He proceeded to the kitchen, opened my wine fridge, transferred the bottles to my nearly empty huge American fridge-freezer and then turned the drinks fridge off. Next came the permanently hot coffee maker and the lights which ran under my kitchen cupboards.

"Fair point."

But he was not done.

Russ walked into my unused dining room, isolated the valve for my underfloor heating and closed the door. Back in the hall, he turned the heating thermostat from a cringe-worthy twenty-four degrees to eighteen and sarcastically asked me if I owned a jumper. By then we were back in the bedroom. He pointed at the cups of tea on the bedside table and tipped his head to indicate for me to get back in bed. I did, of course. He was very persuasive and I was smiling. His rant and show had made me happy.

"Right," he said sternly, "that's reduced your bills to about twenty grand a year. You can afford to fuck up your job."

"Wicked. Nice one. So that's one part of my modern affliction remedied. What about the rest of it—the words of compliance, the agreement, the socially expected noise…"

He raised his hand and abruptly left for the bathroom. The shower sounded and three minutes later he was back, smiling.

"I've got just the cure to stop the talking m' lady." He grinned mischievously. "Are there any other odd bodily issues you want to discuss with me?"

I shook my head. "No, I don't think so. But I do have an obsession with individual magpies—you know, one for sorrow, two for joy—"

"Bollocks, I just saw four out the kitchen window—is it four for a boy?"

I laughed. "Oh, and I count the number of vegetables on my plate so I don't get an odd number." Oh, God. I was revealing more of my craziness. "And I am scared of high places in case I jump."

Russ smiled and kissed my hair. "Have you finished your tea?"

"Indeed, I have. Would you care to come here in order that I can be effectively silenced?"

And he did, of course, and my knees made contact with the inch-deep woollen carpet.

The thought provoking interlude made me even more reluctant to go to the office but I was committed and, as I told him, I needed to go out for the morning-after pill anyway. Much to my delight, he promised to wait until I got back. I shoved my iPad into his hand, flicked the modem back on, and suggested he read something or surf the net until I got back. He muttered something about 'stuff to do in the hut' and I kissed him and reluctantly left his ravish-able person in my bed.

Russ

It made me angry.

It made me angry the girl was so close to the edge she was crying over stuff that didn't matter. My dad spoke about this during his rants—the Mammon of commercialised greed he called it. I had absolutely no idea where Dad got his ideas from. Nobody around us was like him and, because I'd always been like Dad, I'd listened and read and learned and, just like him, I was a revolution incarcerated. It was a bad place to be: an educated plebeian, stuck in the no-man's land of morality between those who did and those who profited from the provision made by the people who exchanged their lives for a meagre livelihood.

Dad would hate Livia and say I was a traitorous bastard for sleeping with the enemy. That alone meant we were going nowhere as I couldn't be with a woman who I 'ad to keep from my family. What with being really angry, I decided to get another brew, because tea was lubrication for a happy soul, and read a bit of news on her iPad thing.

It took me about a minute to switch the thing on and four minutes to unlock the bloody thing. To my surprise, it didn't open on a dull financial website, it opened onto a Kindle app. It appeared she'd nearly finished a book by D.H. Lawrence. Lady Chatterley's Lover. For a laugh, I went back to the beginning and started to scan the text. About a third of the way in I wished I hadn't. To cut a long one short, she was a woman of status who was trapped in an un-fulfilling relationship with her infertile fella. She wanted more, she wanted excitement, and she took a fancy to the groundskeeper on the estate where she lived. He wasn't up for it. He liked his peace and he'd been shat on by his ex-missus. But she wouldn't take no for an answer and she bagged him with her sadness. And the story got worse. She had no intention of leaving her safe relationship, but she wanted a baby and decided the bit-of-rough gardener would give it to her.

Fuck.

The work of fiction was scarily close to my world of facts.

I threw the iPad on the bed and my mind put two and two together and came up with a definite five. That Kieran bloke was the world's greatest suitor and they always seemed close when I'd seen them before me and her. And then there were the things he'd said to me: 'choosing' somebody who works a stone's throw from her house and the comment about 'when all is done'. *Shit.* Livia was over thirty, her biological clock could be ticking, and perhaps he couldn't father a child. She'd coerced me into unprotected sex, not that it took much, and the morning-after pill could be total bullshit. Her getting the pill could be a lie. I'd been set up.

I knew I wasn't good enough for her world and it seemed as though she was playing out her fantasy book with me. For fuck's sake. I didn't need to finish the book. I knew what would happen. The decent, poor gardener would fall in love with the lady of the manor and get her pregnant. She would drop him like a stone and return to her life of riches and he'd be out of a job for his behaviour. Fuck that. She would destroy me. I was already in deep. I needed to do one.

I decided to do a few jobs in the hut and go home. I'd got some holidays owed so I wouldn't have to see her until the dust had settled.

Livia

I wrapped up the meeting in record time; the estimated two hours was crammed into forty-five minutes and the trip to the pharmacy and shop next door went like clockwork. I had never been so happy to be opening my front door and then sad to be met with the furry face of my dog and that alone. I exchanged my trousers for jeans and socks and, leaving a perturbed dog grimacing at the door, jogged down to the hut in the hope Russ would be in there. There was no sign of him and so I trudged back to the house wondering where the hell he was.

Just as I crouched down to scratch Edmund's head, I noticed my iPad and a piece of paper on the island. I grinned—a note, no doubt an explanation about doing something in a sheep field or digging a quick hole. I unfolded the paper.

Oh no. No. No.

Liv, sorry, I wanted to stick around to face you but I haven't got the balls. I've decided to let you get back to your rich businessman and not cause any fuss. I suppose neither of us told the whole truth—it was always going to come out sooner or later. Take care.

Russ.

My legs lost substance and I slumped to the floor, my arms curled around my knees, and my head hanging low. Edmund tried to nose his way in but I didn't let him—I didn't want anybody.

I didn't understand. I had always been totally honest with him but clearly, he hadn't with me; perhaps he had a girlfriend or even a wife. I just didn't know. All I knew was how to cry and get pissed, look after my dog, and then cry and get pissed some more. Fragments of me were falling to the floor and they fell and fell until I felt there was nothing left: nothing but a blur of numbness and indifference. And I was glad of the numbness and indifference because, for several days, it offered me respite from the gnawing pain inside—the pain which told me he was gone and there was no reason to go on.

Chapter 14

Livia

All eyes were on me: me and my six-hundred-pound trouser suit. Beneath the suit was a silk slip and lingerie which cost more than the average weekly wage. Then there was my skin—soft, tanned, and massaged with lotions. Below that were toned muscles and bones and then there was the centre.

I was a Russian doll.

Before I met Russ, I believed I could open the successive layers, every one varnished and adorned with a smiling face, and reveal the final solid, sturdy, doll in the middle; but, right then, I realised that inside the final wooden shell was a void. With Russ, I felt the nothingness recede but he was gone and I realised the extent of my emptiness. I was bereft.

I needed Russ but he was out of my reach; I didn't have his telephone number or know where he lived. As such, I had no idea how long it would be until I saw him again, if indeed I ever did. I wanted to explain; I needed him to explain—all I had was the sketchy note next to my iPad and the rest was assumption. I was lost.

"Livia," the M.D. curtly said.

"Sorry."

I smiled weakly and turned my nauseous, shaky body towards the wall mounted screen. It was only a presentation and I had done hundreds before—I took a deep breath and forced myself not to cry.

"Riding out market instability," I began, with the realisation that the market could be in freefall for all I knew—I hadn't studied the FTSE or checked out my stocks and shares app for days.

I recited my bland words as my mind wandered along with my eyes. The huge table was polished to a shine and around it sat my manager and sixteen influential clients, including Kieran. They, like me, were scrubbed and preened and they presented considered expressions which guarded their thoughts. I hid the quivering hands behind my back and delivered the talk. I handled the questions, accepted the applause, and returned to my seat.

The canapés arrived, along with more drinks, though I ate nothing and sipped at my water. I avoided eyes and conversation. I felt insular and alone. The people at the table chewed the cud as they drank and nibbled and I struggled to stop myself staring into space. I couldn't do it anymore. I couldn't find the pieces I needed to build my stage face; I couldn't muster the energy to even try.

I glanced at the water tumbler and the flute containing something bubbly and very expensive. I took the tumbler and turned it and I was certain there was a tiny particle adhered to the inside of the glass—something which had been baked on in the dishwasher probably. And then I felt really sick.

"We need to reduce the number of cars on the road," the man opposite chirped; "sometimes commuting is nigh on impossible and then there are the environmental impacts."

I took heed and grimaced inside; my cars were an environmental nightmare.

"But vehicles are vital to the economy—manufacture, service, and then there's the revenue from fuel," somebody replied.

The gentleman beside me turned his glass in his fingers. "I think it's time we enforced restrictions such as those in Singapore—no cars on the road that are, say, older than seven years. That way, we keep the new car industry turning over, thin out the traffic, and improve the air quality. We also drive the people off the roads who cannot afford to buy new vehicles— limiting their mobility is sure to be beneficial."

My lip curled. "Do you honestly think that physical freedom should be the privilege of the rich, Liam?"

He smiled, clearly thinking I was being provocative for a debate. "I think keeping the boy racers and people who drive rust buckets off our roads can only be a good thing—they're the people who damage our nice cars because they don't care about theirs."

"Nonsense," I snapped. "What a sweeping, discriminatory comment. Value is relative—an individual earning twenty thousand pounds a year who drives a car worth five thousand pounds would not value their car less than somebody who earned two-hundred-grand a year and drove a car worth fifty—it would probably be quite the opposite."

Liam's brow formed a little arch. He was mocking me and I felt like telling him to go fuck himself. Russ would—in fact no, he wouldn't, he would make a return that unlike mine, wouldn't make people look at me like I had lost my marbles. I shot to my feet and placed my napkin on the table. All eyes turned to me.

"Excuse me."

I smiled thinly and tottered out of the room. I couldn't go to the bathroom. Because strangers visited the toilet. They touched things. The whole place could be riddled with disease. I needed to get out. The carpet in the foyer snagged on my heels. The door took an age to revolve.

I stepped outside and the cold, fresh air hit me. I pulled my jacket sleeves over my hands and leaned against the railing. My bottom lip wobbled, I could no longer withhold my tears. It had all gone terribly wrong.

"Livia, are you alright?"

Kieran's voice was soft, deliberately quiet, not gathering attention.

"Yes."

Nodding uncertainly, he rubbed my shoulder. "Are you tired?"

"I'm fine."

I looked at his shoes. Expensive. Polished.

Kieran sighed. "Livia, what you said in there—is this silliness because of the folly with the gardener?"

I met his eyes and glared. "Silliness?"

"Yes." He made an eek face. "It's very out of character for you to be spouting such words in front of important people. Are you unwell?"

"Perhaps I am tired."

He inched closer and took my forearms in his hands. "I have a squillion airmiles to use and I have a friend who owns a house on the banks of Lake Garda. Why don't we take a few days out?"

"Thank you, it's a kind offer, but I don't want to."

"Why? Won't he let you?" he mocked.

I inhaled and blotted my tears. "He won't care—he's dumped me."

He pulled me in for a very rigid, very brief hug. "Hey, ho. Easy come, easy go. I can't believe you're upset over some illiterate manual labourer— you are silly."

I sprang away from him and grabbed the railing—ignoring the bacteria and spores and toxins which could get through breaks in my skin or cause some horrendous life-threatening allergic reaction.

"He's not illiterate and I'm not silly."

Kieran chuckled. "Sorry. Are you sure you aren't unwell? You haven't eaten anything or touched the Prosecco."

I could have told him it was because I was back to hating the thought of finger food or that I'd whipped myself into a frenzy about what was in the glass—but I didn't—I kept it brief. "I feel a bit off it—I've felt sick all afternoon."

I had actually felt nauseous all day every day since Russ abandoned me—but I didn't tell him that.

"Perhaps it's something you've eaten?" he asked, his voice taking on a 'concerned' tone.

I shook my head. It was because I was devastated. I felt like I had been given the world and had it snatched back and I didn't want to go on. I didn't want to be the Russian Doll who was empty inside: I wanted to be a person of substance like Russ.

"I took the morning after pill—it's probably that."

His jaw dropped. "Jesus, Livia—I can't believe you would have sex with somebody like him. I mean the others, Jason, Aaron—they were respectable men—but him. Bloody hell," he cursed. "And the morning after pill! Did he buy the condoms from out of the back of a car?"

"We never bothered—I didn't want to," I admitted.

Kieran put his strong arm around my shoulder—like a brother or an advisor. "Livia. Go to the clinic, get the all clear, and then come to Garda. Please. Have some time out. You work so hard and you're under so much pressure. We're friends and friends look out for each other. This behaviour is not normal. Arguing with clients. Silly comments. Unsuitable partners. Unprotected sex..."

"Are we friends, Kieran? Just friends?"

His mouth twitched. "Livia, we know the score—we always have. We happen because our circumstances would not suit partners. I put my work before my child, my friends.... it was work which finished my marriage."

Kieran was a Russian doll just like me; inside him was ambition and ambition equated to selfishness—he would never give his last few pence to charity, no, he'd seek a way to turn the charity into a money-making scheme.

"We better go back inside," I interjected. "Could you please give me a few minutes to powder my nose?"

He nodded. "Livia, I'm sorry if I was a little harsh with you. Would you object to a very early morning tomorrow?"

"Why?"

My mornings had started at five since Russ dumped me anyway; as well as not sleeping, I'd taken to running my legs off before work.

"You know how I have a bit of a hot air ballooning habit.... well, my man is flying from the farm adjoining your estate tomorrow. Anyway, I've paid for the basket because I don't like to share with strangers but you're not a stranger. Go on—by way of an apology and to cheer you up. It's a five-thirty start but I'll bring breakfast."

I'd never been in a hot air balloon. But Kieran. Gosh. I didn't want Russ to return to work and catch me with him. Not that I thought it was likely at that unearthly hour. My head was spinning. I didn't want to offend Kieran and it was a nice thought. And, after all, Russ dropped me without so much as a proper explanation.

"Okay," I told him; "and thank you."

Kieran kissed my cheek. "It will be my pleasure. I'll be at your house just after five. I don't like to see you unhappy, Livia. Now go to the ladies' and tend to your make-up. Your hair is looking wayward too."

But I didn't want to powder my nose. I wanted to cry some more. But I didn't because if I started I feared my tears would never stop. I looked to the sky, the clear, starry sky, and I crossed my fingers. Perhaps Russ would come back if I wished hard enough.

Chapter 15

Russ

I sat on the sofa, my elbows resting on my open legs, and stared into the cereal bowl in my hands. Four Weetabix, half a pint of milk, and a good sprinkling of sugar. I wanted to throw up—I couldn't face eating.

I felt shit.

Absolutely shit.

I saw it coming but I still felt like I'd been hit by a train.

"You eating that, bruv?"

I turned to meet the face of my eternally optimistic brother.

"No," I said to Zac.

He took the bowl from my hands, took a pew next to me, and looked me up and down. Black trousers. White shirt. Black socks.

"Who died?" Zac quipped, stirring my breakfast into a grim slop.

"Nobody. Job interview."

I could feel his eyes on my face.

"T—bro—don't do it. You know what they say—act in haste and all that."

I gave my brother a look of disbelief. "Says you. Mr shoot from the hip!"

Zac chuckled and put my empty bowl on the coffee table. "Yeah, I know, but as the fastest cowboy in the west, I'm well qualified to advise you. I'm 'ere to make the mistakes so you don't have to. You love your job. Don't give it up cos of a woman. I assume the posh bird has dumped you— that's why you wanna leave?"

"Just drop it, Zac. It's complicated."

He eyeballed my untouched brew. It was no longer steaming and the milk had split on the surface—it was probably on the turn. Still, he grumbled about wasting tea so I told him he could have it.

"It always is complicated wiv you, bro," Zac went on. "It's much easier to sort stuff out if you do things my way. She asks you how many kids you want, run like Usain Bolt. He finds out you've been doin' his missus, run like Usain Bolt..."

"You find out she's missed a period..."

Looking sheepish, Zac placed the empty mug on the table. "Where's the interview?"

"Garden centre. The one on Beech lane—with the picture of the leaf on the sign. And can I borrow your tie?"

"Yeah, course. Though you might have to dust it off—not had a court appearance for ages!"

I said thanks and groaned as I got to my feet. I really did feel shit.

"T," Zac said, as I reached the door, "don't go to work at a corporate garden centre. Don't sell out. Don't get penned up, tearing yourself up inside cos of frustration. Go back when the dust has settled. She might even realise she fucked up and ask you to come back."

The bile climbed my throat. Having a crap job couldn't tear me up inside because I was ripped to shreds already. "I walked from her, bro. She's with the rich bloke—the geezer we saw her with in the bar that time."

"Has she told you that or av you caught em at it?"

My stomach churned; the thought of her being intimate with him made me want to vomit and then punch a wall.

"Neither. It all dropped into place. I found this book on her iPad—about some rich woman who starts shagging her gardener cos her fella is infertile."

"Ha ha ha," Zac chuckled.

I glared at him—it wasn't funny.

"Yeah. She kinda coerced me into a load of unprotected sex and..."

"Ha ha ha," he interrupted; "oh fucking hell...pussy whipped..."

"Do you want me to break your face or carry on?"

"Sorry youth," Zac uttered. "Go on."

"She said the rich guy was her escort but he told me it was bollocks and they went on holiday together and she took him to her sister's wedding and stuff. And then the night I went to the restaurant with her friends... I don't know...."

Zac grinned. "Have you asked her, straight out?"

I shook my head.

"Well you should. P'raphs the rich guy is being spiteful, and anyway, dig in as the second fiddle and she might even drop him for you... if there's a god."

"Zac, you ever loved a woman?"

My brother's eyes ran along the wall. "Yeah, just the one, loved her for years—still do. Elizabeth—the little blonde girl who works in the Spar."

I was taken aback. I knew her—she was in the year above Zac at school. Quiet. Good at maths and science. The only person I'd ever met who was a vegetarian.

"I thought she was married? Have you? Are you?"

"No. I haven't. I'm not. And I never will," he told me.

"Why?"

"Cos she's fuckin' sweet and she's all fucked up in the head. She needs somebody who's predictable and reliable. Not some fly-by-night maverick like me. I call in to see her on a Monday mornin' and a Thursday night. I leave it there."

"And there I was thinkin' you went all out for self-gratification," I said, dryly.

"P'rhaps I'm not as selfish as you thought. And just to prove it I'll make you a couple of slices of toast to eat on your way out—you can't turn up to an interview with your stomach growling like a bear."

Zac was right about the protecting the girl thing: I loved Livia and so I needed to leave her to the better life and walk away without a fight.

I felt bad, really bad, but, eventually, I knew I'd be alright.

Because I wasn't from a place where they built people out of plastic and printed circuit boards. I was made out of steel and coal and people like me didn't break when we got pushed over; we swore, brushed off the muck, and got back up, lesson learned... or maybe not in my case.

I didn't say anything. I didn't want to talk about her. About us.

And so, I stomped upstairs and went on the hunt for the tie.

Chapter 16

Livia

I watched it take shape with a smoked salmon and cream-cheese bagel in one hand and a very large coffee in the other. It lay on the grass before it fluffed up like a patchwork pillow and gathered the buoyancy to head skyward. Having a huge tower of contained air looming over us made me nervous. I felt so small and helpless and I hoped the balloon ride would be as 'brilliant' as Kieran made out.

"Oh my gosh, Kieran, it's massive!"

"Nice of you to notice," Kieran returned bawdily.

The thought of being intimate with him made me shudder; it seemed so wrong and so alien—like it all happened to somebody else and not me.

Joe, the balloon owner and pilot, strode towards us with a beaming smile. I warmed to him from the off. He was in his late forties, wore walking trousers and a non-matching chequered shirt, and he was passionate about his hobby/job—not because it made him money but because he loved flying. I pulled the wrapper back around the bagel and crammed it in my pocket— I didn't fancy it anyway.

"All ready to go?" Joe chirped.

I downturned my mouth. "Erm, yes, I suppose so—as ready as I'll ever be."

Kieran marched to the basket and clambered inside.

"Don't worry, there's a step in the Jeep," Joe said, gesturing to the nearby Land Rover.

I acknowledged him and smiled, before dutifully hopping onto the step and climbing into the basket. *Shit.* It was a basket: a wicker bloody basket. In my head-up-my-arse mind I assumed that the 'basket' was a figure of speech and we would be standing in some high-tech metal alloyed affair— such as the ones people used for cross-continent record attempts. Joe adjusted a valve or two and the burners roared into life; they were louder than I expected. Kieran hopped from foot to foot and grinned like a child as 'ground crew' freed the ropes and the balloon began to lift. Slowly at first.

Nice and slow. He took my hand and pulled me to one side of the basket, whereupon he leaned over the brim and watched our ascent and I stepped back and took a deep breath.

"Joe," I said, over the roar of the burners, "where are we going to land?"

"We've not even got up yet!" he exclaimed. "And we land where the wind takes us—to a certain degree. You can't steer these things: we're at the will of the gods—we can go up and we can go down. We estimate our direction and speed and aim for one of the pre-determined landing sites." He nudged me. "Don't look so worried."

"I'm not," I lied.

Kieran pulled me to the edge of the basket again and, gripping the top like my life depended on it, I peered over the edge.

"Look, Liv—there's your car."

And indeed, it was my car and it was getting smaller and smaller. *Oh, hell.* The slight sway made me feel like I could fall over and the sense of ascent dropped boulders into my stomach. What started lifelike changed scale—first to big toys and then to small. I wasn't sure—I wasn't sure at all. Kieran urged me back to the edge and I tried to share his enthusiasm as he pointed out the manor disappearing into the distance and then the town appearing into view. I shrugged from his grip and stepped into the middle of the basket. I could feel the anxiety; my hands were shaking; I felt dizzy.

"Livia, come here," Kieran instructed; "you can't see very much from the middle."

I smiled weakly. "No, I'm fine here, thanks."

"Stop being silly," he returned.

"Are you alright?" Joe asked.

"Yes."

I was. Just. But I was sick of Kieran dismissing me as silly and my rationality was slipping through my fingers. The mental justifications were starting; the basket would not break; the balloon could not pop; there was nothing to crash into—the planes were too high and the buildings too low. *Hell.* We were very high. I could see for miles and, while the world looked pretty, it meant if I fell out of the basket…

"Are you sure you're alright?" Joe asked again.

"Yes, yes. I'll be fine. It just feels much higher than it is," I replied.

He nodded, unconvinced, and pulled the lever to make the burner roar once more.

Kieran's joyful expression changed to one of disapproval. "You have got to be joking, Livia?"

"What?" It was a rhetorical question—my hands were gripped tight in my lap and I knew my face was the colour of a frozen turkey.

Impatiently, he pulled me to standing. "Stop being so silly. Stand up and watch."

I struggled from his grip. "I'll look when we are coming down to land— when we aren't so high."

"For the love of god," he huffed; "what the hell is the matter with you?"

"I'm scared," I admitted.

He tugged me some more and I pulled back like Edmund did when I reached the door at the vet's. I had visions of him letting me go and me snapping back like a stretched rubber band and careering over the side.

"Stop behaving like a child—look over the edge and get over it."

"Kieran, get off me."

Joe touched my shoulder. "Stay in the middle with me, love. You can see enough."

"No. Stand with me and stop being pathetic," Kieran snapped.

"I know; I know but…"

He wasn't Russ. What he said. What he did. If Russ was there I would have admitted my unhealthy thoughts and he would have guided me through them. And if I couldn't shed those crazy ideas he would have sat with me, held me tight, and missed the whole balloon ride if need be. I sat back down and Joe told me he would let me know when we were on the descent.

The next thirty-minutes lasted forever and I was very glad when I got the nod that we were going down. I stood up, in the centre, focusing on the sky so I couldn't get a feel for the height, and slowly, very slowly I peered out. By the time we were fifty meters from the ground I was near to the edge, clinging on for dear life, and looking over. I was pleased. So very pleased. We went up, along, and down safely and I decided I might be alright if I went in a balloon again. Regardless, I was more than happy when my feet touched solid ground and less than happy when Kieran, in a strop, stomped off to converse with the guy who drove the Land Rover with the large, rattling trailer.

"Is that better?" Joe said, from behind.

I turned to meet his face, all weathered and mapped with smile lines.

"Oh, gosh, yes—not that I didn't enjoy the flight," I lied. "I think I'll be alright on the next attempt. I got there in the end…shame I couldn't man up in the middle!"

"Hey, Livia, I plan to fly from the farm quite a lot during the next month. If you fancy another shot at it, give me a call and I'll make the arrangements. Did you enjoy it when we were coming down?"

"Yes, I did." *For the few minutes before my anxieties got their claws into me.* I thanked him warmly and went to my unsympathetic friend.

Kieran glared at me. "What the hell was that, Olivia?"

"I got frightened, Kieran—and I'll give it another go."

And I would; Russ had made me realise my monsters were not monsters at all and I could tackle them one-by-one.

"Well, don't think you're coming with me—you nearly ruined my flight."

"Sorry. Is there nothing you're scared of?"

"No."

"You're a liar," I replied. "Failure, Kieran—you're scared of failure."

"I don't need to be scared of failure. I won't fail. People like me never do."

Kieran and I never exchanged cross words and his tone was very indicative. Dismissive. Lacking in compassion. And I didn't want to be near him—not that I told him so. I said that I was sorry, thanked him for breakfast and the opportunity to fly, and put my running shoes to use along the bridal way back to the manor. I needed to get home: I needed to get home to stroke my dog and have a good cry.

Chapter 17

Russ

I pinched one, two, three, bloody loads of dead heads from the pansies while I waited to be called in; it was a force of habit. The gravel crunched and I turned to see some bloke striding towards me, his round cheeks glowing, with a massive grin on his face. He held out his hand. I held out mine and looked at the pile of brown petals in my palm.

"Ha ha," he laughed. "You must be Russ. I'm Elliot. Elliot Scott. Manager. Follow me."

I balled up the petals and tossed them into a flower bed. There were two women standing nearby, green t-shirts, black cargo trousers, toe-capped boots. The blonde one smiled at me and I gave her a half smile back. She was pretty. About my age. I hoped the girl wasn't around when I was released from my interrogation. I'd seen that look before.

The manager dude pointed over the way. "The small log cabin is my office."

It wasn't a log cabin—it was a big shed. The sort of shed a fella's dreams are made of. A rust-spotted convection heater hung from the wall. A drink's station sat in the corner. The kettle was plastic and green. I was made up when my Mam and Dad got rid of their plastic kettle. I didn't like plastic—didn't believe it wasn't a slow road to cancer—thought it should be banned.

He told me to take a seat, offered me a drink of water, and started to leaf through what I recognised as my CV. Blah. Blah. College. Work experience. Level three health and safety. All I could think about was her. And him. What if she was pregnant? What if she hadn't taken the pill? I didn't want my child being brought up by another bloke. I wanted to cry.

"Russ."

The guy's voice pulled me from my miserable thoughts. "Working with the public?"

Didn't want to do it. Hated it when I did it before. Was tempted to reprimand customers about their bad attitude and lack of manners on a twice-daily basis. And I had serious issues taking orders from some jumped-up manager who I could think under the table. Not that I told him that. I needed a job. I couldn't face seeing Livia and I certainly couldn't face seeing her with him. Yeah, the pompous twat was right: she shouldn't have messed with somebody on her doorstep.

"I worked at a supermarket while I was at college. I can say please and thank you and I get things done. I've been doin' a manual job for ages and I can lug stuff around. I'll be useful," I told him.

"Why do you want to leave your current job?" he asked.

"Cos of the travelling. My car broke a couple of weeks ago and it's a right pain cycling to work and back. It's the same money as here and this place is only ten minutes from my house and on a bus route."

And I'm in love with a woman who lives there.

"Why do you think we should employ you over the candidates who have more experience working with the public?"

I raised a pathetic smile. If he looked around his corporate garden centre he'd know the answer.

"Cos judging by your sorry stock, it's about time you stopped employing shelf stackers and employed somebody who knew about gardening. Garden. Centre. The clue is in the title."

The manager smiled and headed into a ten-minute ramble about sick pay, the provision of work clothes, and holiday entitlement. And then he asked me if I had any questions. I told him no and, much to my utter fucking horror, the look on his face told me that job was in the bag and it would tip the scales where leaving the manor was concerned. I shook his hand, he told me he'd be in touch, and I left.

As I got to the car park, I spied the blonde girl from earlier; she was standing by a Ford Fiesta, kicking her feet, and she smiled when she saw me.

"Hi," she said, coy as anything.

"Alright." My feet ground to a halt.

She was pretty, really pretty. Her eyes were a crazy colour of blue and there were freckles on her nose. I'd always liked freckles.

"I just erm," she stammered. "I'm Sallyanne."

"Russ."

"How did it go?" She looked at her toes as a band of red hid the freckles.

"Alright. Not bad. Ta. What's it like workin' here?"

The girl, Sallyanne, twisted a chunk of hair around her finger. "I like it. I only work two days a week though—I'm at college. The people are really nice and they do great cakes at the tea shop. I erm, well… I just wondered if you, erm, wanted to go for a drink. I can't believe I'm doing this… erm, if you've got a girlfriend it doesn't matter…"

"No, I've not got a girlfriend. And thanks—I'm flattered—I really am, but if I get the job, it's not a good idea to mix, you know, work and women."

And that I knew. Did I. I was running away from my dream bloody job and begging for employment at a corporate garden centre because I'd let that woman under my skin.

"It's my last week," Sallyanne blustered. "I've got a work placement at the hospital until next September and then I go fulltime at University—I'm starting a nursing degree." Her eyes darted between me and her car. "I better go. And good luck. If you fancy that drink give me a call."

Sallyanne passed me a piece of paper she had rolled and folded until it felt thin.

"Bye, Russ. Nice to meet you."

"Likewise," I told her, and crammed the note in my pocket.

I headed up the lane, kicking at stones, and my phone rang before I'd made it to the bus stop. No surprise, it was Elliot offering me the job, and I told him I'd talk to the estate manager and then tell him when I could start.

Start. I was back at the start. Again. My life in the gutter. My soul in a tornado of shit. But I'd sort it out—I always did.

The bus appeared on the main road and I stuck out my arm. Luckily for me, my best mate Abraham hadn't got a good days' work in him and so he'd be in for a good blether. Not that I wanted to talk to Abraham about Livia, or anything for that matter, but he'd talk to me about all manner of random shit and I didn't want to be on my own. And then Zac would be home from job club and that was one day dealt with. One day of many. It was going to take tens, hundreds even; and then my deep down sensible voice told me I would never get over her and I could well believe it.

Chapter 18

Livia

I pressed the entry code and scurried in through the narrow metal gate at the bottom of the walled garden. After creaking on its hinges, it clanked and shut out the world—not that it offered me any comfort—everywhere felt prickly and cruel in my state of mind. The entrance meant my tired legs wouldn't have to walk the half mile to the front gates; it also took me within an arm's reach of Russ' hut. The fact was a two-edged sword—it offered a slim chance that I would see him but a high chance of the flailing disappointment when I did not. It had been weeks since I'd seen him at work and I was beginning to think he'd left and our paths would never cross again.

Or perhaps they would.

The door was ajar and I could hear clattering coming from inside. I tapped on the door, walked in, and was met with a face heaving with expression. Russ looked different. Not only was his hair trimmed and styled but he'd clean shaved too. I wasn't sure if I liked it.

"Hi," I said, anxiously.

Russ stared at the far wall. "I don't want to see you, Liv. Just leave it yeah. What's done is done."

I noticed the large bag on the floor into which he had thrown a scattering of tools.

"Why are you packing your stuff?"

He blew out. Hard. "I'm leaving. Handing my notice in on my way home tonight."

"Er, what, no, why, where are you going?"

"I can't stop here, with......I went for a job interview at a garden centre a few miles from home. They said the job's mine if I want it."

"I don't want you to leave." The pressure started to build behind my eyes. I took a few steps towards him and then froze at his force-field of frostiness. "What happened, Russ? I thought everything was good. And about hiding the truth? What lies have you told me?"

"None."

"I assume you have a girlfriend and she found out about us."

He shook his head definitely. "You assume wrong. There's no girlfriend, Liv. I'm no cheat. I've been lying to myself, that's who—I'd actually got it in my fucking head I meant something to you."

I felt a glimmer of hope inside. "You're everything to me, Russ. I don't understand. Do you think I've lied to you? Why are you so angry with me?"

Russ turned to me; he looked hurt and angry—yes, very angry.

"I've been well and truly 'ad. You can't expect me to be happy about it."

"I don't know what you mean?"

"Kieran," he said.

"What?"

He glowered, looking fit to explode.

"Liv, don't treat me like I'm stupid. Did you take the morning-after pill?"

"Yes, of course I did. Where's all this come from?"

"I trusted you, Livia. I let you in, but it seems I'm your game. I'm your bloody gardener—you've conned me into your bloody rich woman, poor gardener fantasy."

I made the iPad-reading material association and smiled. And then I realised he was not joking.

"I haven't conned you and I only got the book because Ellie took the piss when she heard you call me m' lady. I'm telling the truth."

"I'm not interested in your lies. I think Kieran is firing blanks and that's why you wanted me. Till you were up the duff anyway," he said, bitterly. "I've been working odd hours so I didn't have to see you and I was here at five the other morning—as was his Range Rover. Why the hell was he at your house at that time in the morning if he wasn't in your bed?"

"He wasn't in my bed. Kieran has never slept in my bed. He was there at that unearthly hour to pick me up—for a hot air balloon ride to cheer me up after I cried and cried and fucking cried at a business event last week. I'm not with him, Russ. I never was. And he has a child—a little girl called Esme. He's not infertile."

"Are you telling the truth?"

Nodding, I wiped my eyes.

"Yes. I promise. Please don't do this—please don't give up on us. I need you, babe. I need you."

I asked over and over if he believed me; I was near on begging for his acceptance. Eventually, his features softened.

"I'm sorry, Livia. I'm sorry for accusing you of something on a half-arsed whim."

"You're not my game, you never were. Why don't you come and meet my parents? If I was playing you I wouldn't involve them. Please. I've taken you out with my friends. I want to meet yours. I want to know everything about you."

I knew I was making a noise but I blethered on regardless.

"Livia, you can't meet my family or friends. It's the harsh truth. Even if you weren't just shagging me for sperm, it means we're going nowhere."

Yes, and on that I was crying again. "Why? Are you embarrassed of me?"

Russ shook his head. "No. It's complicated."

"It can't be. Unless you are going to tell me you're married with two kids there is nothing that'll scare me away. Well? Have you got a wife?"

"No. No wife. No kids. But I come from a rough place and you'll run a mile."

"I won't," I told him.

"Livia, aside of the book and Kieran, I did a runner to make things easier. We won't work. We can't work. I don't care that your friends slated me the second I walked out that restaurant. I don't give a shit they looked at me like I was the latest freak show. I can take the snide comments and shitty looks but you can't. You're not strong enough. I don't want you to get hurt and I don't want you to destroy me when you drop me down the line."

"I won't, babe—I promise. You walking out on me hurt, Russ—it hurt so much… it still does. Please, give it a go."

He huffed. "Fine—have it the hard way. It's my Mam 'n Dad's anniversary next weekend. Come with me if you're so bloody insistent."

Russ dropped his backside onto the claimed-from-a-house-clearance armchair and put his head in his hands. I gingerly walked over, knelt in front of him and squirmed forward as he sat back. I lifted the bottom of his t-shirt, nestled my cheek onto his stomach and threaded my arms around his waist. Relieved didn't come close.

He lifted my face.

"I've had a jumper on all day—the t-shirt's clean, Liv."

"I prefer your skin." I stroked his stomach with my nose.

"Liv, we're making a mistake—we ought to cut the ties now."

"No. We're not. Mistakes don't feel like this—you know they don't."

Russ caught me by the tops of my arms and pulled me onto his knee. The ancient chair groaned and we waited with baited breath until we were sure it was not going to collapse. I snuggled against him and placed a soft kiss on his neck. And there we remained, cuddled up on the chair, sharing a scattering of words and the odd kiss between the comforting silence.

Russ seemed in no hurry to move but I needed to take a shower and feed the dog. I asked him to come back to the house and he followed without protest. Russ was clearly happy to be reunited with his furry friend but not half as happy as Edmund who jumped around like a spring lamb with a line to the nearest pylon. I broke up the reunion and passed Russ the bag still containing the things I bought him from the shop. From inside, he pulled two new pairs of boxer shorts, two pairs of socks, a t-shirt, toothbrush, and a can of deodorant.

I pulled an eek face.

"Wondered if I could persuade you to stay tonight?"

Yes, we were but an hour into our reconciliation and I was being very presumptuous, but my bed was so barren without him and I wanted him back in it.

Russ grinned. "S'pose so."

I jumped to his side, having well and truly caught the spring-in-your-step bug from Edmund, and squeezed him around the neck. I had regressed, totally and utterly regressed to a fifteen-year-old girl with her first boyfriend. Not that I could continue with my teenage excitement for long because I needed to take the dog for a quick walk before it got dark. Russ said he would cook us an early dinner and I kissed him again. I'd found him, got him back, and he was cooking. And all was good with the world—very good.

I got back to the house a little before dusk, chilled by the autumnal air, and starving hungry having not eaten since breakfast. In spite of the darkness, the only illuminated lights in the house were in the extractor hood and a small lamp in the lounge. I wondered how the hell he was preparing food in a dark kitchen, and when I realised the kitchen was empty, I wondered how the hell he was cooking food at all. I removed my coat, gloves and wellies, washed my hands, and followed the clues to determine his whereabouts.

Russ was kneeling in front of the roaring fire, swirling the contents of a heavy-bottomed frying pan. There were two plates, a bag of prepared salad, and knives and forks on the side table. He replaced the pan on the hotplate on top of the burner and sat beside me as I perched on the sofa.

"Thought we'd have a cheap night in. We can turn the lamp off when I'm done cooking."

In the time it took me to walk my dog, he had made a fire from the 'decorative' piled logs, chopped up the ham from my fridge, beat half-a-dozen eggs, and was cooking a fluffy omelette on the stove I'd never considered as a method of heating, yet alone cooking.

"I can't believe you made a fire!"

He looked at me, bemused. "Can't you make a fire?"

"Wouldn't know where to start."

Russ laughed. "Then I'll teach you how to make a fire. And use an axe. Because, when society crumbles and falls—which it will—being able to use a computer won't mean shit. The people who can find food, make fires— and who know the purpose of a coat," he teased, "will be the ones who survive."

It was a fair point—not that I fancied my chances with an axe…

Before long, my legs were curled under me on the sofa and I was eating by firelight.

"Liv," Russ said, sounding uncertain, "I wasn't prying or owt, but when I was looking for the salt and pepper I opened this cupboard and… Jesus, babe, do you actually take all those tablets?"

I chopped the last piece of omelette with the side of my fork and put it in my mouth. I was not even tempted to lie or make excuses.

"No. I gave up on the amitriptyline after a week because I felt like crap in a morning. I stopped taking the sertraline because it gave me terrible headaches. The doctor gave me the course of diazepam because I couldn't sleep—I saved a few in case I got desperate. I only take the natural stuff now—the St. John's Wort in the day and the Calms at night. Yes," I said, smiling; "take one pill popping happiness fraud…"

Russ took the empty plate from my lap and placed it on the coffee table. He shuffled between my knees and gathered my hands.

"Take one pill-popping happiness fraud, add one scruffy gardener with seventy-two pounds to his name, and what do you get?" he asked.

"A bin full of tablets and a hope and a prayer."

And I knew, I knew right then, that me and Russ, our conflicting worlds reverberating due to their near collision, were meant to be. I'd previously thought it incomprehensible to be sitting in such an unconsidered state; my face was clean of makeup due to my earlier tears and my windswept hair was even messier due to Russ' attempt to 'turn me into a wildling' because he liked me looking 'feral'. There was no TV. No internet. No mobile phones. No music ringing out from the CD player. Everything was perfect and, for a moment, I wished I'd never taken the morning after pill.

With the heating off the rest of the house soon dropped cold—not that it mattered as we decided to get the duvet and pillows off my bed and sleep on the rug in front of the fire. While he stoked the log burner to last through the night, I undressed and snuggled down under the covers. I watched as he whipped off his clothes and he teased me and said I was a 'perv'. I replied that I wanted to watch because he was 'as hot as fuck' and he laughed and asked me to say fuck again. I said the word and wrapped my legs around him as he kissed my smile.

With everybody before Russ it was just sex but with him it was different, heavy with feeling—we held hands and watched each other as we kissed. We shared our bodies. And so much more. Our words. Our thoughts. Our time. Losing him was so painful but getting him back was finding the end of a rainbow every minute—and I wanted to feel every minute before it raced by. We were two people stripped of difference and the layers of expectation, enjoying our time together. The ancillary materialistic bullshit which had, and still, supported every other relationship in my life were absent—with him they were unnecessary. He was a complex, amusing man who could obtain contentment without the gratifying career or the lavish possessions. Russ was complete: a person who, rather than needing to have, just needed to be. Right then, beneath the warm, orange firelight, it no longer mattered what I owned—it was more important who I was. I wanted to be a person and not a magnet for materialism; I wanted to be happy and I would never be happy without him.

And that simple, cuddly night was the best of my life.

Chapter 19

Livia

Yet again, I left work on time that evening. Since I met my intriguing gardener my working habits had definitely improved for the better as far as I was concerned. I was taking the next day off as Russ said he was taking me away for the night. I was clueless as to where but I was as excited as a child, not only because of the trip but because, what with him attending a forestry course for work, I hadn't seen him for two days.

"Hello m' lady," he said, grinning broadly. "Your carriage awaits."

Rather than simply returning the hug he gave me, I attempted to squeeze the life out of him. Yes, the playing it by ear was much better than the social air kissing.

"You fixed the car, big man?"

"Nope. Lent me Dad's. Have you packed your bag?"

I nodded.

"Got your dog?"

I loved how Russ considered my dog and me as part of the same package. Kieran saw him as an inconvenience—he never even stroked him and the concept of bringing him on a romantic night away would be totally unconceivable. I patted the grey, tail-wagging ball of stupidity which appeared at my feet and nodded again.

"Well come on." He tipped his head to the door. "Let's go and fetch tea. I sorted the accommodation this afternoon."

Much to my delight, but not total surprise, dinner was not at a restaurant or even a pub. The ritual started by waiting in a queue under florescent lights, gazing into the glass, heated cabinet. I could not decide. Fish or pie, fish or pie, fish or pie. *Ahhh.* It was our turn and so I went for the obvious: the one best accompanied with an eye-streaming dose of vinegar. Given the choice of meal, I was glad I added a big packet of baby wipes and foaming hand cleanser to the pants, toothbrush, bed socks and dog bowl he suggested I packed.

I'd come on leaps and bounds with the hand-hygiene OCD, but leaving home without a method to cleanse my hands was still too much to contemplate. I also packed facial cleansing wipes, a small bag of make-up, a hairbrush, deodorant, nightie, dental chews for Edmund, dog biscuits and, against Russ' wishes, my mobile phone. Oh, and the KY jelly went in there too—just in case.

On his insistence, we got the fish and chips to take-away and I juggled them on my knee on the short journey to our destination—the plantation at the very top of the estate where a tent had been pitched and a fire, a boy-scout would be proud of, constructed a little way from it. Edmund leapt from the car and began sniffing out foxes, and I was as happy as Larry too.

Russ lit the fire and got fold-up deck chairs out of the boot, and I chose the place where I could best supervise the dog in his crazy schemes, watch the crackling fire, and eat fish and chips until my giddy heart could take no more. There was even a flask of tea in the car to wash it all down.

It was wicked.

Russ was in a really talkative mood and he told me of his plan to look into the Open University and start a degree. He talked about his horticulture diploma and how he mainly did it to get him outside and away from people. I said he was antisocial; he said he had good reason. I asked him if he had girlfriends at college and he said just one, dismissively told me it was in the past, and asked how many past loves I'd had.

I let out a little laugh. "You won't believe this, but until I was thirty-one I'd never loved anyone. I dated a few blokes at University—Scott was the longest and I quite liked him. Peter was a laugh but I fancied him like a kick in the head. The longest relationship as a post-grad was three months. Yeah, I'm flighty," I added, grimacing. "I dated a guy on and off for about three years after I started work but dumped him when he wanted to get serious. Then I got Edmund and he filled the company void so I just had fling after fling. They never worked as everybody wanted commitment, and that's when I landed on the idea of an escort."

"So I take it you met Kieran and fell in love at thirty-one?"

I shook my head and the words just kept coming; I assumed there was something in the Yorkshire teabags.

"Oh no. I started seeing Kieran when I was twenty-eight, twenty-nine, and I've never loved him."

I could hear the cogs turning as he assimilated the timeline.

"When's your birthday, Liv?"

"About six weeks ago."

Yes, about the time I met you. I had said quite enough. Russ grabbed my gloved hand and pulled it onto his lap. His hand covered mine, the fingers resting in my palm, his thumb crossing my knuckles.

"It hasn't taken us long to climb so high 'as it, babe."

"No." I smiled shyly. "But you know what they say about climbing high."

"Yeah. But who gives a shit about falling when you've got a parachute."

"And have you got a parachute?" I asked him, knowing that I certainly hadn't.

Russ sighed. "Nah. Don't suppose I have. It could be one hell of a splat on the floor!"

I laughed; it was a good way to divert a tricky conversation. We could not be talking about love—it was too soon—but as much as we tried to pretend we didn't notice, the tension kept popping up and telling us it was there. The stupid, irrational, foolhardy thing that it was.

I squeezed his hand and gazed past the twisting, bright fingers of the fire and out into the dark. In the distance, I could see the manor house; a bright cluster of yellow-white lights, sectioned away from the madness of the world with its single arterial road. Beyond the manor was the illuminated network of roads, sparse around the edges but becoming denser towards the centre like sparkling dew on a futuristic spider's web.

Two months earlier, I would have not set foot up there. The blackness would have consumed me as it pulled at my insecurities and fears; the thought of being without a mobile phone reception, the central heating, running water, and even a toilet would have been too much to take. But, with Russ, I was without concern. He felt earthly and grounded and I got the impression that, if he was cast out of suburbia, he would be quite happy in the middle of nowhere. I suspected his beard would grow long and thick and he would make do with stream water and a weekly trip to stock up at

Aldi and see his friends and family. I wasn't even panicking that I could no longer see the freaky, green reflective eyes of my dog.

Everything seemed simple. We both needed food, drink, warmth and shelter; perhaps we weren't so different after all.

Russ let out a shrill whistle through his tongue and teeth. I tried to copy, liberating a sound like a destitute house sparrow, and I suspected the dog was sitting at our feet in a flash due to his effort and not mine. Without a shadow of a doubt, my most loyal companion had taken to his new keeper nearly as much as I had. I reckoned he liked the quiet; away from my constant jabbering and fussing he could get on with being a dog—dossing like a dog, sniffing about, spending all day mooching in a field following rabbit trails.

I got the impression it was getting late and it was definitely getting cold; our breath shot into the sky like silvery tracers and the fire was dying down.

"I'm going for a pee before I get undressed and warm in the sleeping bag," I said; "if you hear me scream, make sure the zombies haven't got me."

Russ chuckled. "The zombies aren't up here, babe, they're down there in suburbia watching reality TV. Now the rabid badgers on the other hand...they'll see your bare arse at fifty feet!"

We all three went our separate ways to empty our bladders before piling into the tent. Russ produced a tube of toothpaste and we brushed our teeth and spat the bubbles in one of the empty chip trays. He then wrapped all of the rubbish and put it in the car 'cos of the foxes'. Minus a few clothes, Russ and I climbed into a sleeping bag he made by joining two others together, and Edmund curled up by the door with a dental chew.

Russ turned off the torch, we cuddled together, and I wrapped my smooth legs around his hairy ones. And what followed was by far the worst sex of my life. It was even worse than losing my virginity. For starters, the sound of a mutt grinding and crunching his way through a bone a few feet away from our ears was not conducive to romance. But still we pressed on, too tempted by semi-naked bodies and raging hormones to stop. The intimate togetherness of bodies was soon replaced by hands, and before long he disappeared into the sleeping bag and I was breathing heavily, and verging on orgasm. And then there was the pad, pad, pad of claws on the plastic groundsheet and I could smell the bloody dog before he arrived at my face.

"Edmund. Get back down there," I cursed, not impressed as my climax petered away.

"Babe," I whispered into the nylon shell of the bag, "come up here."

I pulled on his hair and urged his face back to mine. Soon we were kissing, yes, kissing without anxiety, and I touched him until he pulled my hand away and attended to the contraception—yes, I needed a period so I could get on the pill. I struggled to free my leg in the confines of the bag and liberated it just enough to get it around his back to pull him even closer.

Crunch. Crunch. Grind. Choke, bloody choke!

I reached out and grabbed the torch, pointing it at the stupid dog that had literally bitten off more than he could chew.

"Oh shit, shit," I panicked. Russ was out of me just in time as I lunged out of the sleeping bag, my bare arse flashing in the air as I crawled down the bed. My eyes grew wider and my hands flew to my cheeks—afraid to touch the dog for fear of making it worse. "Do you think he's going to choke to death?"

"Nope," Russ huffed; "I think he's gonna cough 'til he's sick."

He scrambled out of the bag, his bare arse joining the line next to mine, opened the tent door and shoved Edmund outside. And he was right, of course. A minute later, the dog had been sick and was lapping at the bowl of water as he banged the shell of the tent with his tail.

"Av you done been a pain in the arse?" Russ grumbled at the dog.

Edmund wagged his tail even harder, plodded back inside, and curled up in the corner of the tent. I shut the door, told Edmund to go to sleep, and crawled back into bed.

"Right then, where were we?" I flirted.

Russ climbed into bed and told me right back before the start. At first, I wondered what he meant before I straddled him and realised the dog vomiting had definitely been a turn off. But not for long. Within seconds, I was making use of his virility, and we were kissing until we couldn't breathe. I sat up, he touched me, and I failed to hold back long enough for him.

"Oh, for fuck's sake!" he exclaimed.

And the expletive wasn't because of an earth-shattering orgasm.

A few things do not simply smell repulsive: they are intolerable. One of them is cat food, another is vomit, but at the top of the pile is dog fart. I was off the man and opening the tent flap quicker than it takes an electron to circle the atom. Russ was not far behind me, sticking his head outside and sucking in the air like a man half drowned. Edmund, on the other hand, was oblivious; he remained curled up and fast asleep, even after I told him the next time he would be stopping at home or going to the RSPCA.

By the time we rested our heads on the pillow, the tide was well and truly out; and if it wasn't so funny I would have been devastated that, for the first time ever, my partner had not climaxed during sex. There was no fake orgasm and no fake apology. We practically, and in a most adult manner, agreed that nobody could stay aroused following exposure to a dog fart. It was humanly impossible. So we kissed and cuddled and soon we were sleeping, wrapped in each other.

Russ

In not so many words she said she loved me. How, why, and whether she was just deluded I didn't know. But there was one thing for sure, I was right there feeling the same. Her and her crying, that mental hair and die-hard allegiance to that stinky dog—who I right liked.

I was not embarrassed of my family or ashamed of my roots, but I wished I'd not said I'd take her home. The last time I took somebody special to where I lived, it signalled the beginning of the end of a very precious relationship and it nearly destroyed me. And I was really scared the boundary between our worlds was too big for Livia to cross too. Livia was not the girl who I first met—fidgeting, counting, and freaking the hell out at every opportunity—but it still took very little to send her running for the hills of anxiety. Prejudice. Roughness. Anything nonconcrete, i.e. my fecking life. And as for the running, if she did one, I knew she'd run straight back to Kieran.

Livia would hate where I came from and would never see me the same again. Where I came from and what it made me would ruin everything. It had before and it would again. And if my brother put his charming fucking presence into the equation—I wasn't going there.

Taking her home would put me in the shit too. Livia represented everything my friends and family hated. Corporate. Wealthy. Stuck up. My Dad was going to flip. My Mam would probably cry. My friends would probably spit in my beer cos I'd bailed on my morals. But fuck it. In my eyes loyalty came above all and if they wouldn't respect my decisions then they weren't with me. End of.

It was three-am but I was wide awake, listening to Livia's little breaths and Ed's annoying snoring. I tossed and I turned but it was no use. After deciding that frustration is enough to kill a man, I ran my hand from Livia's waist and along the soft flesh of her hip. She'd put on a few pounds—probably because of the world-class food I'd introduced her to—like fish finger sandwiches and Yorkshire puddings with golden syrup. I curled my hand around her hip; there was definitely some more padding around those bones and I liked it. I liked it a lot.

Livia stirred with a purr and a tiny groan.

"What time is it, babe?" she said, her voice all husky and hot.

I hitched her top leg to waist height and pressed the knee to the floor. And then I spooned in real close behind her.

"About three. But I really wanna make love to you."

Livia wriggled back to meet me and I kissed her between the shoulder blades. She let out an 'ahh' and squirmed into the position I absolutely loved.

"Hmmm," she returned. "Sleepy, soft, and gentle?"

"Yeah. Really sleepy, soft, and gentle. Somewhere we've never been."

Livia turned her head and her languid lips met mine.

Yeah. Somewhere we'd never been.

Chapter 20

Livia

I was as nervous as hell—so jittery I had a sly shot (not three drops, but an actual shot!) of Bach's Rescue Remedy to settle my nerves. Russ was due at any time to direct me to his house and I was looking forward to seeing him so much.

Russ and I had had a wonderful week; he stayed over four times and we took turns doing breakfast in bed before I dragged my reluctant ass to work. My past assumption that we wouldn't have much to talk about quickly went out of the window. Tea (to add milk at the beginning or the end). School dinners. Brexit (don't get me started). Organic farming. Politics (we agreed to disagree). It went on and on. Russ was smart—crazy smart. Opinionated and up for a healthy debate. Well-read. As dry as the Sahara Desert. And he could cook. He opened my eyes to culinary pleasures such as toad-in-the-hole, baked rice pudding, stew and dumplings and, my personal favourite, fish finger sandwiches—which I'd even craved at breakfast.

We'd had a brilliant time when we weren't intimate and a brilliant time when we were. Things with him were unlike they had been with everybody else. It started with the very first kiss. No awkwardness. No mismatched rhythms. Everything was perfect. There was no ritual or expectation, and no going for three straight sixes from the judges. Sometimes it was earth shattering and twice, quite frankly, it was cringe-worthily terrible. The first attempt in the tent was bad but being bent over the island and forgetting the bacon was under the grill was ridiculous. As was the ensuing small fire and the ten minutes it took for the air to be clear enough for the smoke alarm to stop screaming. But it didn't matter. We simply laughed it off and started again.

Laughter, for the first time since I was a twenty-year-old undergraduate, was something which happened several times a day. The twenty-minute drunken discussion about custard turned into stand-up comedy. And I could do nothing but laugh after I lost at Hangman because I failed to get 'The Financial Services Authority'.

Not only did Russ magnify my good moods, but he knew how to diffuse my bad ones too. The night I arrived home from work, as stressed as hell, he messed up my hair, kitted me out in his clothes and said, 'I declare this woman an office free zone'. And on that, I handed him my phone and laptop and all was perfect: real, technology-free, and perfect.

Russ was right all along: a daily overdose of endorphins and the newly rediscovered serotonin from plenty of sleep were starting to ease the anxieties I thought were around for ever. Russ brought me peace, smiles, and above all perspective. I was seeing the world outside my work—in fact I struggled to see the work through the world half of the time. What I saw was with a new perspective too. I still met people in their expensive suits, those whose scent lingered in a room long after they left, but they appeared different: they seemed to be made of stuff that was cheap and would fray to nothing if you found a loose thread of question and pulled. But I had hope; because, for the first time since I became a teenage girl in my private school, I actually felt like I could take away the clothes, the hair, the makeup, and the reputation of professional excellence, and there might be somebody worthy inside.

Edmund rushed to the door and whined and I followed him—walking and not whining, obviously. My stunning, if ruffled, accomplice arrived on foot and it appeared, for once, he hadn't been stubborn and got a lift considering there was no sign of his bike.

I was somewhat confused when Russ instructed me to park at the local Morrison's and called for a taxi to take us the last five miles of the journey. Then, as the miles rolled and we edged closer to our destination, I realised why. It soon became clear that we were heading to an 'estate' I had heard discussed but to where I'd never ventured. According to rumour, the emergency services didn't even go there without a police escort and, undoubtedly, neither of my cars would have lasted ten-minutes parked amongst those streets; I assumed that in a deprived area a fifty-grand Porsche would be vandalised and an Evo stolen. Though they were the thoughts of the discriminating person who I clearly was; Russ came from the estate and, days previously, I offered him the choice of both cars, no strings attached, and he adamantly declined the gift and, with a cheeky smile, asked if he could have my dog instead.

Yes, my method of prejudice was not failsafe.

The infrastructure seemed to have a grim will of its own: a grimness which sapped more colour from the world with every rolling yard. Street after street of grey pavements were fringed by concrete-shelled houses; some tidily kept, some weathered by years of poverty, and the occasional one, devoid of inhabitants, had metal shuttering on the windows. One house stood proud, the lawn neat and the drive gravelled, ashamed of the grimy house and the wayward garden beside it.

I stared out of the window, trying to hide the disheartened look from my face.

"I said you should've never come," Russ uttered.

I shot him a plastic smile and squeezed his hand. He was no longer gripping mine tightly, it was almost as though he was letting me go.

"I've never been here before," I returned, as a lacklustre diversion.

"Yeah and you'll never want to come 'ere again. It's a bloody shit 'ole."

Russ asked the driver to stop, paid up, and said we would walk the rest of the way. I had noticed him glancing at the rising red 'fare' numbers as we travelled; I knew that Russ didn't have much money and he would rather hand over his shoes than accept mine.

And so, we began our deliberate steps along the dismal pavements.

"I could've cried when I 'ad to come back here with my tail between my legs," he told me.

"How long have you been back home?" I enquired, inwardly shuddering at the implication of what his 'home' would be like.

"About six months—just before I got the groundkeeper job. I left when I started college. I was working at the supermarket so I rented a room in a shared house before I got the flat with Nicole."

My stomach tightened; I hated the thought of him with anybody else and he definitely spoke her name in a way which was laced with regret and not bitterness.

"Did you love her?"

"Yep."

I hoped he would follow up the admission with a statement that he no longer did but it never came and its omission made me feel solemn and sad.

My reverie was broken when he manoeuvred me away from a trail of dog excrement. I looked forward to the patches of concrete where the grass verges had been infilled. I tried to hide my distaste.

"Yeah, there used to be trees and grass before the council got rid of them to save money on maintenance. It looked much nicer round here when there was some greenery," he said, almost apologetically.

I scanned the front gardens. Hardcore. Paving slabs. Gravel. On some, the grass had simply been churned to mud by the action of tyres. And there were dandelions. Everywhere. Unlike at the manor where every weed was ripped out and replaced by towering foxgloves. Or brightly-coloured evergreen shrubs. Or expensive fruit trees. Before the soil was mulched over to keep the undesirables at bay.

"I assume she was your girlfriend. You're not with her now?"

Russ shook his head. "Nah. We split up months ago. She saw sense and dumped me."

"Why sense? I think you're lovely."

"I ain't ever been called that before. Oh, come on, Livia. Let's call a spade a spade. I'm not exactly eligible—your parents would never approve of a minimum-wage gardener from a shitty council estate. Even your friends looked at me like I was your experiment when you towed me into the restaurant."

"Don't be silly, you're not my experiment. You know you're not," I said, with the conviction to assure myself as well as him. "Is it far?"

He pulled on my hand and tipped his chin. "We're here."

The path was cracked and broken. The lawn tended but sparse. Russ tested the door handle and, on finding the door unlocked, shoved it with his shoulder. And then he paused, rolled his eyes, and sighed despondently in response to the raucous emanating from the room to the left of the short hallway.

"That you, Big T?" a gruff male voice shouted.

"Yeah." Russ turned to me. "Sorry about this. I hoped nobody'd be in."

He grabbed my hand tightly and led me into the room. The living room was approximately a quarter of the size of mine and the dated furniture vied for space. The floor was covered by a densely-patterned blue-green carpet, that beneath my feet displaying the strings of the backing due to wear. The room was gloomy, a consequence of the small window which was dressed with a yellowing net curtain, and the eclectic mix of old, brass ornaments and cheap oriental crockery did nothing to brighten the ambience.

I was stunned.

I took a deep breath on the realisation that the entertainment was suddenly me. Four young men, in their twenties, were scattered around the room in various states of slobbery. I cast my eyes around shyly. To me, in my little world, seeing a gathering of men in a house without women was most odd.

"Lads, this is Livia. Please keep it clean," Russ implored, before outstretching a hand to point out the men in turn. "My cousin, Ashley."

Ashley was skinny, in his early twenties, and had closely cropped fair hair and beady pale eyes. He intimidated me immediately—what with looking quiet and restrained and with a tendency towards violence. He held his hand up in acknowledgement and I returned a shy smile.

The second character was sitting on the sofa with his denim-clad legs slung over the arm and Russ introduced him as his friend Riley. He was heavily built with spiky black hair, a black t-shirt and black jeans, and he scared me too.

"Alright, luv?" he said, smirking.

"Hi, yes thank you," I returned.

It was not true and I shamefully felt a wall of discrimination building itself, separating me from the coarse reality that was second-by-second becoming the reluctant actuality of Russ' world.

The next in line was a grinning young man with black skin and bleached blonde afro hair called Abe, who it materialised, was the owner of the deep voice. The final guy was sitting on the floor, fiddling with a phone, and only glanced up when Russ introduced him as Alec.

Russ sat me on the arm of the sofa and put his arm around me. "Where's Loki?"

"In t' shitter!" Alec exclaimed.

"I said keep it clean," Russ snapped. "Where's me Mam 'n Dad?"

Through a thick part-Afro-Caribbean part-local dialect, Abe explained they had gone to town to get Margo, his mother, some new tights and 'summut' to wear for the party that night.

Russ caught my eye and the corners of his mouth lifted in a slight smile.

"It's goin' well. We've bin in here two minutes and nobody's said owt obscene."

Riley dragged his attention from his phone. "What—like telling 'er you're really a cu—"

Russ stopped him with a glare; his expression surprised me—as did the fact he seemed to be pulling rank over the bigger, muscly, scary looking man.

"Don't fuckin' look at me like that, T," Riley returned.

"Don't say that word in front of her—unless you want to be shittin' teeth," Russ told him seriously.

Gosh. I didn't know what was going on. I didn't want the big man to fight Russ and I certainly didn't want them to come to fisticuffs because of the use of an offensive word in front of me.

At which point, a stunning, topless, dark-haired man entered through the door opposite; he was the man who had accompanied Russ at the bar. *Hell.* Not only did he have the face to stop women in their tracks, but he had a body which was a bottle of fake tan away from making the front cover of Men's Fitness too.

"How the fuck has my little scum bag of a brother managed to pull a fox like you?" he said.

"Don't start," Russ snapped. He snatched a shirt from the couch and threw it at who I assumed to be his brother. "Get some clothes on. This is Livia—she's cumin to Mam and Dad's party tonight. This is my brother, Zachary."

"Hello, Livia. Nice to meet you. I won't shake your hand or give you a polite kiss cos our kid 'll probably hit me." Zachary slung the shirt over his shoulders. "Where the fuck was you last night? Thought you were cumin out with us lot, T?"

Russ grabbed my hand and urged me to the open door.

"I woz busy."

"Fuckin' bailing on the crew again!" Zachary scoffed.

Irate, Russ turned to his brother. "Zac, I'm not in a crew. And limit the swearin'. There's a lady in the 'ouse."

Zac grinned, right at me, and I squirmed.

"Yeah, I can see that," Zac stated. "I can see why you've bin pussy-whipped."

Russ folded his arms, squaring his frame.

"Now, now, ladies," Abe quipped, breaking the confrontational line between them.

Zac and Alec tittered before Abe told them to stop laughing using no fewer than five informative words and twelve expletives. I cringed at the coarseness of the language and silently flapped because of the tension in the room. I did not like it; I could not deal with situations where confrontation arose out of nowhere and aggression felt within reach. Russ informed his brother we were going upstairs and would see them at the club.

My hands shook as I followed Russ up a narrow staircase. It was dark and dismal, with a threadbare carpet. The estate, the taint of poverty, and the gang of young men had thrown me. And I felt more vulnerable than I had ever.

We reached the small landing whereupon Russ pointed to a door and told me it was the bathroom. Then, to my surprise, he grabbed the long metal pole leaning against the wall and used it to open a loft hatch. He hooked the pole into a silver ladder, and pulled it down.

"After you."

Wide-eyed, I asked, "I assume this is a wind up?"

He shook his head and held out his hand.

Very gingerly, I put a foot on the first rung and started to climb the ladder. On reaching the top, I crawled onto the floor and got to my haunches as Russ emerged and pulled on the light cord.

The middle of the loft had been fitted with floorboards and mostly covered by a piece of carpet; the corners curled, reaching for the sky, and a bright patch stood out, where he'd probably tried to bleach away a stain. In the centre of the floor was a double mattress, to the side of it was an oil-filled radiator, and behind us was a chest of drawers with a small TV atop.

I was totally and utterly stunned.

"Me n Loki always shared a room but he came home first an' there was no way I was going back in with him. So, I came up here. It's alright—I only need a bed and somewhere to keep my stuff. I can't say I'm bothered about luxury and it's only 'til I've saved up enough to move out."

He dropped onto the mattress and patted it, gesturing for me to join him, as a round of hollers came from downstairs.

"They're very rowdy," I said.

Russ nodded. "Sorry, it'll be quieter tonight—there'll only be Mam, Dad, Loki, and whoever he's shagging."

"What happened there—with your brother?"

Russ blew out laboriously. "He woz winding me up—it's just in his nature. Me and Loki are gonna have to have a chat about rules."

"Huhh?"

"I ain't having him looking at you like that. You aren't like the others."

My heart plummeted. Others. I didn't ask because I didn't want to know.

"Why do you call him Loki and why does he call you T?"

Russ chuckled though the weight of issues clearly suppressed his mood. "It's what we've been called since we were kids. You know, Thor and Loki. I'm the blonde good one. He's the dark bad one."

The side of my mouth lifted a little, "As in the myth?"

"Nah, as in The Avengers." He paused, circling his thumbs. "You're shocked."

Shocked didn't come close. I knew his family wouldn't be wealthy after the comment about the washer but I had put them in the 'working class' box. I expected a semi-detached house on a nondescript street; a patch of lawn and a square of decking, maybe; a ten-year old Ford Focus on the drive; a compact, slightly outdated kitchen—self-fitted and purchased from a DIY store; beige carpets throughout—polyester and lacking decent underlay; three bedrooms—his been the smallest and barely big enough to contain a double bed. And as for his parents; in my mind's eye his mother was blonde, like him, not overly clever but nice and smiley, and she hadn't worked since she gave up the job as a dinner lady when her boys left school; his father was tall and sturdy and had been a manual labourer who worked his way up to foreman or something. Yes, I'd thought it all through and a pin had now popped every one of my balloons of prejudice and preconception.

"I'm surprised. You said your parents weren't wealthy, but Russ, I hate to sound stuck up here, but I wasn't expecting this place and I wasn't expecting you being in a gang." I covered my face with my hands. "I'm sorry, I've just never been to an estate with so much erm, I don't know..."

"Poverty. Benefits. Swearing. I never lied to you. I just didn't tell ya I was the only person in the house with a job and probably only one of three on the street. And I'm not in a gang. I keep out of all that since I went to college. Don't judge me, Liv."

"But you even talk differently with them and why doesn't anybody have a job?"

"My dad got made redundant from the lead works eight-years ago, couldn't find a job, and now he's too ill to work. My Mam always worked in the corner shop 'til the Tesco opened and they closed her shop down. She can't work now—she's scared to go out on her own since t' burglary. Loki's not long bin out of prison..."

"Prison?" I interjected.

"Hmmm. My brother has issues with dropping his pants and using his fists. He had a spate in fight club tho' the people he fought never agreed to it. I told you not to come, Livia. I've really fucked things up by bringing you here."

I reached for his hand though I did not meet his eye.

"No. It was me who insisted on being nosy and coming to your parent's anniversary party. Is the pub far? I mean, are we taking a taxi— is it safe to walk around here? I'm frightened for you, Russ. You don't even have a car—you walk and cycle everywhere," I fretted, becoming increasingly worried at the thought of the both of us walking the desolate streets at night.

"The club's about a ten-minute walk away. I wouldn't let you walk to the bottom of my path on your own but you'll be alright with me. I'm Thor remember—I've got a massive hammer," he joked.

I laughed. "Is that what you call it."

Russ scurried to the front of me. "I'm not liking this version of you. I'll get a change of clothes and we can go back to yours."

I ran my finger along the crease on his duvet cover, watching it all the while.

"No. No, absolutely not. It's your parent's party and I need to stop being a stuck-up cow. Well, no, I'm not. I'm just scared and out of my comfort zone."

He placed a single distracting kiss on the side of my lip. "I quite like you being a stuck-up cow."

I pushed him away playfully. "Stop it, the…" I nodded at the open loft hatch.

Russ jumped up, retracted the ladder and, leaning over dangerously, pulled up the hatch. He seemed to be plodding on regardless, ignoring the twitching of uncertainty suddenly residing between us. But I could not because I was dizzied by the harsh, brutal facts of our newly revealed circumstances.

Just the day before, I searched the internet and chose a hotel, equidistant between where we lived and that of my hometown, where I'd planned for my parents and sister to meet Russ and his family. But now… my parents would be horrified when they learned that his father didn't have a job and his brother was a convicted criminal. My family would never approve of us. Never. Ever. They would be ashamed. My mother and father would be disappointed; my sister would think I was having some kind of breakdown or a mid-life crisis. Just like my friends.

And then there were his friends.

I saw how the young men in that room looked at me as if I was some intriguing specimen which had been washed up on the wrong beach on the wrong continent—which indeed, at that moment in time, I felt like I had.

I wanted to battle away the side of him I had just discovered and hold on to the part of him which I knew. I always knew a social rift lay between us though I never once thought it would turn out to be a chasm—a battleground—littered with hostility.

Everything suddenly felt too daunting.

Too much.

And my mind began to stumble.

Chapter 21

Livia

I clung to Russ as though he was my last link to life as we marched down the dark streets. I was glad I had taken his advice to 'just wear your jeans', but was all too aware that my designer jeans came with a hundred and fifty-pound price tag and my 'day-off' boots were the sort of thing people wore to the Chatsworth country fair. Cruelly, and with unwelcome discrimination, the second I entered that living room I knew that everything about me screamed of money and, while clean and smart, the attire belonging to the men sitting in it screamed of a lack of it.

We chatted as we walked and soon Russ pointed out the sign belonging to the squat square-looking working man's club to where we were heading. All in all, it was an uneventful stroll until three young men emerged from an adjoining road and approached us, three-abreast, on the pavement. My heart battered my ribs. I glanced to Russ who maintained his pace and squeezed my gloved hand a little tighter.

"Do you know them?" I whispered anxiously, noting how they paced towards us.

"Not really. Liv, don't panic, but if this kicks off and I say run, run to the club and find my brother or mates, yeah?"

My stomach knotted as my prejudiced fears bombed in. As soon as the taxi pulled onto the estate I became afraid of violence, drugs, gangs, and all of the things I'd seen portrayed in 'gritty dramas' and on reality TV. I had tried to abate my fears and tell myself it was all sensationalist but, as the group of youths strode towards us with their pigeon chests sticking out, I became very concerned that my fears were real.

"Kicks off?" I asked.

"It won't, Livia. I'm thinkin' worse-case scenario."

I went to step onto the road but Russ stopped me. He veered to the inside edge of the pavement, as to be non-confrontational, but they immediately averted their route. And then we were all stationary and face-to-face.

"Excuse me, lads," Russ said politely, and attempted to walk around them.

A youth blocked his way and pushed him in the chest. There was a brief, silent standoff before two of the young men began swearing and saying pointless, aggressive words. One of them pushed Russ again as the others encouraged him to 'knock the cocky bastard's fuckin' teeth out'.

Hands in his pockets, Russ squared up to his attacker, towering over him, right in his face. "Do you know who I am?"

The most forward of the lads, the one with a weasel's face and crooked teeth, laughed out loud. "Prince Fuckin' Charmin'. In fact, hand over your fuckin' wallet and phone."

Russ seemed unperturbed by the fact he was against three others, younger lads, but even so. He pulled off his woollen hat, crammed it in his pocket, and rubbed at his hat-hair. "Right, now lose the beard an' all."

The youth took two steps away and the arrogance fell from his face.

"Worked it out, have ya." Russ glared at them in turn. "So, if you're stupid enough to lay a finger on me, or more importantly her, you better get running because I will catch you, and I will fucking kill you." He pointed at the lad wearing jeans so low-slung I could see his pants. "And as for you. You wanna count yourself lucky I'm wearing my best clothes, or you'd be eating this pavement for swearing at her."

He backed away, muttering apologies. The mouthy one soon followed, and the third, clearly clueless as to why there was a sudden change in play, fretfully asked who he was.

The weasel-faced one muttered Russ' name.

"Shit."

They broke into a jog and headed for the common.

I started to cry; never before had I witnessed, yet alone been involved in such a scene. Russ surrounded me with his arms.

"It's alright, babe. Don't get upset."

"What the hell happened there? He was pushing you about. They were going to mug us," I blubbered.

"They weren't. They'd have to be off their tits or brain-dead to touch me. Don't worry." He wiped away my tears and kissed me on the nose.

"There's only one person I'm scared of round 'ere and we haven't come to blows for ages."

"Who's that?" I fretted. "Will he be out on the streets?"

"Nah, he's already in the club," he said, nonchalantly.

"What's his name?"

"Zachary—my brother. And if it ever kicks off with us, find a wall and hide behind it. Messy doesn't come close when we go at it. Come on, love—gi' me a smile. We can't turn up at a party with you crying."

I was shocked. Stunned. And even more confused. It seemed that my mild-mannered, philosophical therapist/gardener was not only a fringe member of a gang but also had a hard man reputation. And there was something between him and his brother. The day had all been too much and I needed a drink.

Russ led my wavering person through the creaky doors and into the old working men's club. When the place was built it was proud and sturdy; but the buoyant present was long gone, as was the sparkling future.

Dirty brass footrests circled the bar. The chairs were upholstered though the velvet was tatty and worn. The rows of strip lights, the height of fashion in the eighties, had yellowed plastic frames. And the dark-red carpet, originally lustrous, was thinned by the footfall of time.

Worn and weary.

Used and broken.

Just like the working class the club was built to serve: once a hub of power and solidarity, now forced to accept what it was given and abandon all hope.

The people, just like the once showy club, had inherited a reality they did not deserve. Thatcherism. New Labour. The corporate money machine. Decade upon decade of relentless destruction. It was an unwinnable battle, I supposed. Some of the older people looked haggard, desiccated by the loss of prospect. A few had been made shapeless by circumstance. Others bloated by sugar. Many of the younger women were emaciated or made bland by reality TV. And the younger men mirrored their female counterparts; some a pair of sensible shoes and a blazer away from passing as a private school student; others a flick knife or a packet of drugs away from a part in a gang-culture movie. Yet all of them, young and old, cutting a path in the only way which they knew.

Not that I didn't feel scared and intimidated and overcome.

That said, I was captured by the rattling soul of the place. The genuine laughter. The private jokes. The warmth. The comfortable friendships. The way people threw their arms around their partners and nudged their friends. There were pickled eggs and Scampi Fries behind the bar. People crowded around the Pool table or played Darts. A couple of women sported ghastly coloured hair.

To a certain extent, fashion and expectation had left their little niche untouched. Nobody seemed to care that the outside world now nibbled on olives and drank Prosecco—or that leaving the house with hair the colour of a Smurf surmounted to social suicide. And seeing people not cursed with the veneer of the upper classes was wonderful.

Refreshing and wonderful.

We took a seat and Russ sourced cardboard table mats on which to put his beer and my white wine; my glass was dainty and out of place amongst the heavy pint pots, just a small tap away from a big fall. His friends talked amongst themselves and displayed the caddish behaviour I expected from a 'gang of unemployed youths from an estate'—not that I found it shocking or unpleasant—quite the opposite, actually. They were all friendly and welcoming and tried hard to disguise the burden of prejudice that blatantly existed on our opposing sides. Abe was especially cordial and, what with his beaming white smile and loquacious character, I liked him straight away. It transpired that Abe was Russ' closest friend and I stuck with him when Russ excused himself to visit the bathroom, go to the bar, and see if his parents had turned up in the adjacent function room. Zac jiggered off too and Abe and I got onto the subject of my Mitsubishi Evolution and the fact he would love to 'thrash the tits off one'.

"Ah you alright, babe?" Abe asked, as the conversation petered and he obviously noticed the worried look on my face.

"Hmmm. It's the lads who just arrived at the bar. They erm, threatened Russ on the way here. Though they backed off when they realised who he was. Is he a secret hard guy or something?"

"He's not to be messed wiv. It'd take a couple of us big lads to bring him down. He'd make mincemeat out a them three skinny little runts."

"What. How?"

Abe grinned and leaned across the table. "Livia, babe. Russ spent fifteen years fighting his psycho bruver—don't know how their house is still standing or their poor mam coped—but that sorta training kinda shapes a person."

"He doesn't seem the type to go around fighting."

"He's not. Only seen 'im hit one bloke since he woz a teenager. Though he woz the top dog on t' estate and Russ gave 'im a very public shoeing. Painted the pavement wiv his blood. Kinda affirmed 'is status as a very dangerous fella. There aint no little scrotums gonna mess with Russ 'round ere. Not wi his backup an' all."

"Backup. What, you mean you lot?" I asked.

"Well yeah, us 'n more t' point, Muhammad Ali over there." I followed his eyes to Zac, who was standing at the bar, grinning like a fool, as a blonde-haired girl swooned over him. "Nobody messes wi 'im 'round 'ere."

"Ah. His brother. Wouldn't even the 'top dog' mess with him?"

Abe chuckled. "He is the top dog, babe. Loki calls t' shots 'round ere."

I knitted my brows together and tried to drink away the confusion. "But you just said Russ only ever beat up the top dog on the estate?"

"Aye. Only person 'e ever battered woz is brother. Nearly turned 'im into a cabbage," Abe casually said. "Never seen so much blood squirt from a person's face."

"Why would he hit his brother? I saw them in town a few times and they seemed so close."

"They are. Thick as thieves. The only thing that ever come between Thor and Loki wor a woman. And given the event that woz unfolding in the 'ouse earlier...."

Abe flinched as a shoe drove into his shin. Ashley glared at Abe and shook his head in warning.

"What woman? When was this?" I asked, feeling sick to the stomach.

"You better ask 'im," Abe returned. "It's more than me life's worth tellin' you that story. They'd both 'av a go at stringing me up by the innards."

On that note, Zac appeared at the table, grinning like a cat that had got the cream, and asked me why I always looked so worried. I blushed under his inquisition and realised that, in all reality, I probably had looked afraid from the moment I arrived on the estate.

"Oh erm. The three lads at the bar just unnerved me a little. They accosted us and the tall one started pushing Russ about on the way here."

I turned my head to see the grimace that crossed every other face at the table. Zac turned around, acknowledged the young men, and calmly took a drink. A short minute later, he casually got to his feet, approached the bar, grabbed the skinny lad by his collar, and pulled him onto the ground. He then proceeded to drag the youth, gasping for air, kicking and yelling, out of the room. The remaining men at the table released approximately five-hundred expletives, mainly revolving around the words fuck, shit and bollocks, and then, in perfect unison, they pushed back their stools, got to their feet, and ambled out. I sat frozen to the spot, comprehending the situation but unsure as what to do.

"Oy." A kiss landed on my cheek and I as good as jumped out of my paranoid skin. "I was only gone ten minutes—where are me mates?" Russ asked, putting another drink in front of me.

"Erm. Hmmm. I'm not sure but I sort of said that a lad at the bar was among those who threatened you on the way here. And then your brother dragged him out of the room by his throat."

"Oh bloody hell," Russ muttered. "Where are the lads?"

"They followed him out," I replied coyly, cringing at the chain of events I had inadvertently caused.

"Liv, just a tip. Never tell Loki anybody 'as upset me. He's a bit over protective and he's a shit-storm waiting to happen."

"Sorry."

"You weren't to know." He accepted my apology with a full on, beer flavoured kiss. "Come on. Time to go and meet my folks."

A man in his late fifties met me with a stare of distrust as I followed his son into the room. Russ patted the worn cushion on the long seat flanking the wall, and I apprehensively sat on it before he joined me.

"Dad, this is Livia. Livia, this is me dad, Adam."

"'Ello duck."

"Hi."

Adam, Russ' dad, the man standing with his hand outstretched, was not the person who I had envisaged. From what I'd gathered from Russ, his father was a thinker—a philosopher and a seer—and, as such, I had pictured him with thin grey hair, a thick beard, dark-rimmed glasses, and open features. The real Adam had dark hair which was mottled with grey and smartly combed. The sides of his eyes were hatched with the relics of a million smiles and the deep groove between his brows told of a million scowls. His forearms bore patches of faded blue and green—tattoos from years past, their images lost in the blur. Adam did not look like a man who nurtured the wonder of deep thought: he had the sallow skin of a person who'd spent a life indoors and he looked tired and worn. Regardless, it was clear from whom Russ had inherited his steadfast character and unwavering composure.

A few moments later, a short sturdy woman appeared; she had thick calves and saddled hips and waved a small salmon-coloured piece of paper.

She grinned at Adam. "We won! We won the meat raffle."

"Ay, brilliant," he returned, and gave her a squeeze. "What did we win, love?"

"A ham and a leg of lamb. A whole leg, Adam!" The woman, who I assumed to be Russ' mother, turned and hugged Russ warmly. "Did you hear that me little un. Lamb for Sunday dinner!"

Her referring to Russ as 'me little un' warmed me inside; he was six-feet tall and a good fifteen stones. But she clearly doted on him and her husband—who returned her fond looks and affectionate gestures.

The difference between our families was blatant. My parents referred to me as Olivia, in their tight-lipped fashion, and the relationship between my mother and father was icy; I suspected that gin, golf, and a large circle of socially active friends had sustained their marriage for decades.

Russ smiled, broad and deep. "I'm there, Mam. Save me the usual chair!"

For a second, my brain froze in disbelief. A raffle. A meat raffle: a competition where people competed for what I considered staple food items and not hot air balloon rides or cases of Moet.

"Mam, this is Livia," Russ continued. "Liv, this is me Mam—Margot."

"Ello, Livia."

I held up my hand and smiled. "Hi. Nice to meet you."

"I like your dress," Russ said to Margot; "you look nice."

Margot beamed and it was clear that the new cheap outfit and his genuine comment made her happy. Truly happy. The compliment was neither a social pleasantry, nor did it have the intention of false flattery, and the schmoozing people in my 'world' became even more plastic. Yes, they were polished and smiley, but their 'happiness' could easily be a bluff to coerce other people into envy. I wondered how much of a good time anybody was having in the restaurants and wine bars because I, for one, had certainly not been made happy by the charade for a very long time.

Margo gushed and told me I was 'so pretty' and then, to my surprise, said, in all sincerity, that if I caused trouble like his last girlfriend I would have her to deal with. Russ had never discussed her but, reading between the lines, I suspected something had happened between her and Zac and that was the reason for the incident between them. My gloomy thoughts were soon broken by Russ lurching sideward, nearly pushing me from the chair in the process.

"Here you are, T," a sweet little voice exclaimed.

A young woman kissed his cheek before embracing his parents in turn and taking a seat. She too had dropped most of the local dialect like Russ and I felt the arrival of the green-eyed monster as I discreetly studied the new arrival at the table. Tall, slim, and of African-Caucasian descent, she had honey-brown skin that was clean of makeup, large brown eyes, and full lips. She was beautiful. Very beautiful.

"Bev'ly love," Margo cooed, "how long 'av you bin back?"

"A couple of days. Thought I'd pop home to catch up with Russell. Aren't you gonna introduce me, T?"

Russ, clearly ill at ease, sighed. "Livia, this is erm, Beverly. She's erm Abe's half-sister. Erm, this is Livia, we erm, well we erm… We've been spending time together for a bit."

I was disheartened. We had never discussed our relationship but I really wanted Russ to refer to me as his girlfriend and abate my newly emerged insecurity. Not only was Beverly a model, with the face and the figure, but she called Russ 'T'—just like Abe and Zac: people who were significant in his life and who had been around a lot longer than I had. And judging by the way Beverly manhandled Russ, she was more than just his friend's sister.

"'Ow's the modelin' going, love?" Margo asked.

"Good, yeah, good. It's a bit weird with all the travelin' and been pampered and that but I'm enjoyin' it," Beverly chirped. "But I'm done on my year out now so I'm back at uni to finish my degree."

"What are you studying?" I asked, hoping to disguise my discomfort with friendly conversation: the discomfort which magnified following the realisation that Russ did not retake my hand after hugging his 'friend's sister'.

"Oh, fashion design."

"Cool."

"Yeah, it's really good 'n I've got a job to go to when I've dun—some design house who I've bin modellin' for. It's good. What do you do, Olivia?"

The use of my full name grated, along with the reluctance to reveal my profession to his parents.

"Financial stuff. Nothing exciting."

"What like workin' in a bank or summot?" Margo asked eagerly.

"No, erm," I stammered.

"She's a financial consultant," Russ said, and put his arm around me.

Beverly asked what the job entailed as Adam folded his arms.

"I basically manage money—for companies mainly; I make investments, evaluate hedge funds, and move assets around. It's all very dull," I said, willing the questions to cease.

Adam coughed and went on the beer-driven attack. "So, you work for the businessmen and make them more from the money they have?"

I could feel the waves of hostility and reached for the hand on Russ' leg: a move which Beverly followed with her eyes.

"Not necessarily. Often the aim is to optimise asset fluidity or maintain a fund. It's not always in everyone's best interest to be making money on everything all the time."

I wished I had bitten my tongue rather than gush. It was my disease. The modern disease: I had to talk, talk, and bloody talk.

"Funds—you mean like pension pots?" Adam asked.

I released the lip from between my teeth. "Sometimes."

The penny dropped before he continued.

"I 'ad twenty-nine years in a final salary pension. The corporate bastards folded the scheme an' I got advised to reinvest in something what I were told were 'safe'. They said it'd build the pot so I wouldn't 'ave been losing out so much when I retired."

I shook my head sadly. "I know what's coming."

"Yeah. We would've bin comfortable me and Margo if somebody 'adn't put my life savings into some wildcard investments and I wouldn't 'av to rely on the generosity of my son to buy me missus a new washer."

I fell inscrutably silent, vilified by my trade.

"Have you done?" Russ asked sternly.

His dad gritted his teeth and took a large drink of his beer.

"And it's a lovely washer int it, Adam! It's got a quick wash and you can 'ardly 'ear it when it's spinnin'," Margo chirped.

I smiled and had an overwhelming urge to hug Margo and then take her misfortune and hardship away: the hardship which fell upon a salt of the earth woman after the bit of comfort she held out for in old age had been gambled and lost.

Russ broke the tension with the offer of a drink and headed off with Beverly hot on his heels. I did not know what to say and, lost for words, gazed at the bar, my eyes flicking to the aggravation building alongside it. My temporary malaise was broken by Adam's gruff voice.

"It's a shame int it, duck."

"Hmmm?"

He nodded towards the raucous building on the other side of the room. "When you take the power of provision from a man it makes 'im insane. A man needs to provide— it's in 'is genes. Throw all the insane men in a room and all they can provide is an act of faith in 'emselves. And that's when they turn on each other. Black or white. Christian or Muslim. Society educates them and tells 'em the only way to provide is wi' money and they're poisoned from the inside out."

"I never thought about it like that. I'm glad Russ isn't materialistic."

Adam shook his head. "No, he's not. He's a good lad. They both would be given t' chance. I tried to push 'em far away—but they won't go, too loyal for their own good. Especially Russell, me little un. Even when he was with that posh girl he was back ev'ry Sunday."

"What happened with Nicole?" I asked.

Adam's eyes went glassy. "Not for me to say, duck."

I was becoming ever more paranoid about the whole girl issue and I did not like it. I had never done serious, possessive, or clingy, and I was feeling all of those things with Russ and it scared me. He was still raw over Nicole and it was grounding. It was the reason he avoided me like the plague at the beginning and the reason he did not want to take me home to meet his family.

And then there was the beautiful, honey-skinned girl who was pawing him at the bar. He had never mentioned her before and there was something hidden there too.

I felt sick and was unsure if it was the anxiety or the alcohol. I was matching my company drink for drink and they were sinking them like there was no tomorrow.

Adam broke the uncomfortable silence.

"Sorry about gettin' at you earlier, duck. It's the injustice. It eats you. It's 'ard to stop the flow if there's an outlet," Adam woefully said, looking at his hands.

My eyes were drawn to his hands, the skin dry, the joints swollen and arthritic. The first finger on his left hand ended at the knuckle.

"What happened to your finger, Adam?"

He raised the hand and wiggled the stump nonchalantly. "Trapped it under a pile of lead ingots—crushed that bad they 'ad to chop it off."

"That's terrible."

"They brought us up wi' a good work ethic. They never told us the work wud wreck us. Breathin' in muck that knackers our lungs. Doin' jobs that would wear our bones and make us deaf. That's before we did summot stupid and lost a finger," he said, lightly. "And all those bastards did in their ivory towers was polish t' stick to beat us with. I look at 'em young 'uns out there with their unemployment and their benefits, and, as much as I despair, I'm not sure pandering to a different system is any worse."

On deciding the nausea was caused by envy-induced paranoia, I decided to ask Adam about Beverly.

"Russ and Beverly seem friendly."

"Aye."

Margo reappeared, her ears flapping. "We thought they'd be married by now. Probably would be if it wasn't for 'er."

Her. Another referral to Nicole. The situation was really starting to gripe.

"Beverly was 'is first love and he was hers. Lovely lass—int she, Adam."

"Yeah, but just drop it, Margo love. They moved on years ago—nothin' for you to worry about, duck," Adam said, in an attempt at reassurance.

I was not reassured and the continuing presence of Beverly at the bar and the subsequent contributions to the conversation made by his newly appeared brother and friend didn't help either.

"Ya wanna watch my sister around him, babe," Abe quipped.

"Ignore him, Livia," Zac said, with a wry smile; "he's windin' you up so you rip T's head off. He hates the thought of my bruver ever shagging 'is little sister."

Abe opened his mouth to release an expletive before Adam silenced him with a glare. I felt my anger swell and I very nearly swore myself. Luckily for all, Russ appeared with a round of drinks and gave me a possessive hug.

The next hour ticked by and I finished yet another glass of wine. The buffet was open though there was no way, given my rapidly focusing anxieties, that I could eat anything from it. I apologised but, saying I was tired, asked Russ if he would mind if I called for a taxi to take us back to his house. He innocently fed my unhappiness when he said that it was not necessary. I felt it was necessary. I was scared.

A short time later, we left; it was past eleven and the party was in full swing.

"Is this when you dump me then, Liv?" Russ asked as we set foot on the damp grey pavements.

My frostiness had not gone without notice.

"Dump you, Russ?" I asked rhetorically. "You told the pretty girl I wasn't even your girlfriend. Why didn't you tell me the girl who popped your cherry would be there?"

He exhaled woefully. "Livia. I was fifteen—it was nearly a decade ago."

"Fifteen. But when did you last have sex with her?"

My mind berated my tongue as I spoke; I had no idea what the hell was the matter with me. Russ sighed and suggested I stopped spoiling for a fight. I ignored the request and asked him exactly how recently he had slept with her. I wished that I hadn't.

"About five months ago. Bev was my rebound fuck. Happy now?"

"No. Did you go down on her, Russ?"

"Stop it, Liv, sweetheart—don't go there."

I knew he could see the direction of my thoughts and I knew my thoughts were insane. It was in the past and it wasn't like I hadn't ever performed oral sex on a partner. But still, there was no reasoning with my illogical ideas when I was feeling so bad.

"Will she be your 'rebound fuck' when you dump me?" I asked bitterly.

"No because I'm not going to dump you—you're going to dump me." He rubbed his woolly hat. "And with the girlfriend thing—I'm sorry if I upset you—I didn't know what to say. We've never talked 'bout it and I assumed somebody like you wouldn't want anything serious with someone like me."

"And who exactly is somebody like me?"

"Somebody who moves in a privileged circle and brings home more in a week than I do in two months. As if I'll keep you happy for long. I haven't even got a car to take you anywhere. And as for Bev, I'm sorry—I didn't know she'd be there; she's bin abroad for months and she's just a mate."

"Russ, you were standing at the bar with her for ages!"

"I was waiting to get served—it was two deep." He paused for thought and then nudged me playfully. "Liv, are you jealous?"

The comment hit me right where it hurt. I was jealous and I hated it. At the beginning, I thought we would only be a fling, men always were, and it concerned me we had very quickly turned into something else.

"Me! As if I'm jealous of some giddy girl who can't say 'g' and who fell lucky and got her arse off—" I stopped abruptly. *Some scummy council estate.*

"No, go on," Russ urged, his words laden with offence.

"Sorry. You have so many secrets; I don't even know you."

"You know what you need to know, Livia. I'm the same person I was yesterday. I take it you've dumped me now you know I'm not middle class and come from a shitty housing estate?"

"How can I dump you, Russ? I'm not even your girlfriend."

The house was in darkness and the swollen door took a lot of persuasion before it opened. Amidst unspoken words, alcohol induced frustration, and frayed tempers, Russ directed me to the kitchen so he could get us a glass of water. Walking in, I noticed the bright white washer standing proudly besides the yellowed fridge and the electric cooker on which the rings were made of black spirals.

"Why have you and Zac got good teeth?" I asked cryptically. "I think I only saw four good sets of teeth all night."

"Are you pissed?"

I nodded. It was true—the world was starting to spin and my mind was flitting with uncontrollable thoughts. My re-emerged OCDs were clawing at my sanity and, as I noticed the higgledy-piggledy jars on the kitchen side, I started to worry about the cleanliness of the glasses from which I had drank all night.

"Most of the older ones had 'em pulled because it's cheaper than getting em fixed. The younger ones all had dummies when they were little. Mine are straight cos my Dad made me have a brace. Zac always had straight teeth—not that they're 'is teeth now, the front two are capped—he got his kicked out."

"God, that's awful!" I exclaimed. "Was it you?"

Russ headed to the hall, locked the door, and marched upstairs.

"Who told you?"

I followed him into the bathroom where he splashed his face and got his toothbrush.

"Nobody. I assimilated the clues. Apparently, you kicked the shit out of the 'top dog' on this estate. A bit later it was suggested that your brother ran the streets around here. What happened?"

Russ spat the remainder of the toothpaste in the sink, passed me his toothpaste-recharged toothbrush, and told me to turn around while he 'had a piss'.

I started gathering the visual fodder for my increasing anxiety. I saw the tidemarks of damp around the rotten wooden window and the tile grout which was discoloured with patches of grey mould. And then I noticed the round tap which I could not turn off with an elbow. Neither the tap nor basin appeared dirty but I could sense the bacteria and I wondered how many young men had been to the toilet and washed, or not washed their hands in that bathroom. I needed to pee but I couldn't sit on the toilet seat and did not want to go through the shame of hovering while inebriated with Russ in the room.

Russ did not tell me what had happened and so I pressed on.

"Was it something to do with Nicole?"

He did not answer the question and hadn't returned a response by the time we got in bed. I asked him over and over and, with equanimity, he told me to drop the subject which, obviously, only made me more persistent.

"You still love her."

"No. I don't."

"Then why won't you tell me about her. I'll tell you about any of the men I've been with—I don't care."

Russ put his hands over his face as he dropped back on the pillow. I was weeping through frustration and the more he skirted around the issue the more important it became.

"Secrets, Russ. I can't stand the secrets."

"Fine," he snapped. "I'll tell you my secrets. I hit fourteen and became a hormone filled, risk-taking fucking nightmare. If it wasn't for the fact I've grown a brain, I'd show you my Free Running—there isn't a roof for miles I haven't climbed on. My life was like Tekken and for two years 'police' and 'caution' were always said in the same sentence. It was a miracle I got my GCSEs 'cos I got kicked out of school. It woz a bigger miracle I finished college 'cos I spent the first year so hammered on Es and Speed I could 'ardly remember my name. Yeah, I live on the scummiest, most notorious council estate in the area. My parents are unemployed, my father despises everybody, and my mother—who I love dearly—is one of the dimmest people I ever met. My brother is an ex-convict and a Lothario. My friends dabble in drugs and gang warfare. Beverly doesn't want me for a boyfriend but she's never shy about the fact she always wants me to shag her. Will that do?"

"And will you shag her?"

He shook his head. "No."

I wanted him to say more but nothing was forthcoming.

"What about now—do you still get in trouble?" I asked tentatively.

"I don't involve myself in any of that stuff. The lads know to keep me out of their crap. I spend my nights watching telly and reading." He nodded at a precarious pile of thick text books and well-thumbed paperbacks in the corner. "I'm bettering myself. Carving a decent future. I want out of all this."

"Drugs?"

"Not touched em since I met..."

"Nicole. What exactly happened with her?"

He did not answer my question but instead glared at the wall. I crawled out of bed, got my underwear from the top of the drawers, and started to dress.

"Fine. Fucking fine. I loved her; I thought we were gonna end up married with kids but she screwed me over big time. Now just leave it and come back to bed."

I looked to the un-plastered ceiling and took a deep breath.

"Please," he said, softly.

I nodded.

I did not want to leave him.

I wanted him to wrap me up and show me that everything was okay: that we were okay. I pulled off my jeans and slung them on the clothes rail in the corner, knocking a pair of black trousers onto the carpet in the process. With my head spinning and body swaying, I snatched them from the floor and returned them to the plastic hanger. As the metal hook went 'cling', a piece of paper fluttered to the carpet. I picked it up and unrolled it.

It would be great to see you again.

Phone me.

Sallyanne x

Below the girl's name was a telephone number.

"Shit," Russ uttered. "It's not how it looks."

I turned to him, shaking my head in disbelief. "I'll take that as an admission of guilt."

He pulled the hand from his hair and ran it down his face. "It's not—it was a stupid thing to say. I haven't been out with her. I didn't ring her."

"I take it they're your interview trousers. There I was—totally fucking dumped and barely holding it together—and you were happily hooking up with somebody else."

He got to his feet, looking defensive.

"I never hooked up with anybody. I was just as cut up as you—I never called her."

"The note says 'it would be great to see you again'. So, you just went out with her once?" I yelled.

"No. I never went out with her at all. I met her at the garden centre—when I went for the interview. She asked me out. I said no."

"Then why did you take her fucking number?"

Russ shrugged. "I don't know. Politeness. Guilt..." He took a deep breath. "I haven't done ought wrong. You're pissed, Liv—things 'll seem different in the morning."

But I could not wait to find out. Russ was the anchor for my sanity and, with the doubt surrounding him, I could not hold on. I knew I was being irrational but my brain was in chaos—kicking out and telling me to run. I couldn't see the wood of logic through the trees of his secrets. Women here. Women there. A past he had buried. A present he'd tried to hide. A cataclysm had torn up my mind, bringing with it an incoherent mess. It was all there, at once: the bacteria on the bar of soap in his bathroom—the hands which dipped into the bowl of peanuts which Russ ate before kissing me—the stomach-churning notion that his mouth had been between Beverley's legs.

Panic. Panic. Fucking panic.

The socks Russ had discarded were odd. The line of toiletries on the floor was disorderly and not in the order of size. I raked my eyes around the room and began to furiously count. Seven jumpers on the rack. Thirteen DVDs in a pile.

Shit. It had happened: I had finally snapped. I needed to go home. I needed to get back to my antibacterial cleaner sprayed taps and the glasses which had been in the dishwasher at eighty-five degrees. I needed the comfort of my tested smoke alarms, the fire doors and the three routes of escape. Before him, I was barely holding it together in my sterile world and, after everything, I had totally lost it in his tainted one.

"I'm sorry but I can't sleep in this roof. I'm worried about getting out if there's a fire. I'm even scared of falling down the ladder if I need to pee in the night."

"Are you serious?"

I nodded woefully as I slipped on my coat. I could not talk to him as I could not find the words. I needed to run away from the realisation that just as Russ had the power to heal me, he had the power to annihilate me too. He implored with me to stay before calling for a taxi, slipping on his shorts, and accompanying me downstairs.

"Oh for fuck's sake," he yelled, as he burst into the living room. "You've got a room. Use it!"

I immediately realised the reason for his outburst. Zac was sitting on the sofa and the blonde girl from the club was kneeling before him. I could not believe my eyes; I actually saw his penis and her mouth—it was like being in Amsterdam watching some tacky sex show. Zac stood up and pulled up the trousers and boxer shorts from around his ankles, and the girl rose from her knees and wiped her mouth. Having just got a glimpse of real life porn, I could hardly believe my eyes. That was absolutely not my world and I had an overwhelming urge to run fast and far.

"Another one bites the dust," Zac said, obviously piqued by the intrusion.

Russ glared angrily. He appeared to be on the edge of an emotional cliff and not in the mood for provocation. "What's that meant to mean?"

"Well, the lovely girlfriend was stoppin' over, now she's goin' wi' tear tracks down her face. Perhaps you ought to stop punching above your weig…"

Russ' fist met with Zac's face. I froze in shock, my hands on my cheeks and my mouth agape. I thought being up close to a live sex act was bad but it was nothing on the scene of violence which unfolded before I'd drawn breath. The girl screamed as Russ threw Zac against the back of the sofa, and punched him, over and over. The sofa tipped over and Zac turned on Russ. I shouted for them to stop and rushed over, intending to intervene, before retreating, petrified. There was no pushing, shoving, and noisy punches like I had seen in the movies, just brutal fists, jarring joints, and the sickening thud of bone meeting with bone.

And then, the front door opened, and in marched a determined man who bellowed at the top of his voice. Russ and Zac separated, their chests heaving.

"You are grown men," Adam yelled, "an' I will not have you actin' like animals under my roof. What's 'appened now?"

The brothers looked at the floor, dabbing their bleeding, rapidly swelling faces.

"It'll be over her," Margo sobbed, accusingly pointing at me. "Time repeatin' itself. I knew it would soon as I saw 'er. Only a woman 'd come between them two."

Adam threw his hands in the air. "Well? 'Av you touched 'is girlfriend, Zachary? Cos if you av I swear I'll kill you myself."

"No," Zac exclaimed vehemently.

"Ever touch her and I'll kill you, Zac. I'll do it next time," Russ barked.

The sound of a car horn sliced through the night.

"My taxi," I muttered; "I better go."

"Yes, I think you better 'ad," Margo said.

I raced out of the house without a backward glance.

Chapter 22

Russ

Livia walked out and there was Zac's blood on my hands. Again. I could not believe I'd been stupid enough to let it all happen. I should have ignored the thing which was between us right at the start. I should have never kissed her in that bar. Straight from the off, I knew I would shatter her illusions and she would shatter mine. Because I would never be good enough for Livia.

I left the house, not in the mood for round two or another bollocking from Dad, and there was only one place I could go. Abraham's. I'd been best mates with him since I was six. Back in the days when people were ignorant and stupid enough to tease a kid because of the colour of their skin. Never bothered me—stuff like that never had.

I hated how those grim streets felt beneath my feet. They pulled me down on their patchy, grey tarmac—telling me who I was and staking their claim on my soul. I wanted to leave; I wanted to stay. I hated the bitterness and the poverty but I loved the grit which made the place. Rejected. Resented. Carving an existence out of nothing. I stretched the ten-minute walk out to twenty and arrived at the council-issue new red door on their shoddy house.

"Av ya killed 'im?" Abe asked, flinging back the door.

I followed him into the dingy hall and squeezed past the wall of coats. "Nah. I hit 'im tho."

"As she dumped ya?"

I nodded. "I reckon."

"Sorry, man," Abe said, the words stretched and warmed by his Afro-Caribbean lilt.

"It wor inevitable. Are you gettin' that kettle on, Abraham?"

Abe nodded and I leaned against the kitchen side and watched him perform the ritual of making two cups of tea from one teabag, the norm in his house. They all did it: him, his mam and Beverly. They would put the teabag in one mug, fill it right to the brim, let it stew, and then pour the tea between two cups—only fishing out the teabag and topping them up with hot water at the bitter end.

He passed me a mug and I sauntered into the living room. The lights were off and the only illumination was from the TV and a paused game of FIFA. Abe sat down, hitching an ankle to the opposite knee, and I took the sofa opposite. I quickly established that the rest of his family were at the 'lock in' at the club and I was free to talk.

"Has Zac shagged her?" Abe asked, going straight for the kill.

"No."

"Then why 'av you 'it 'im?"

I scuffed up my hair. Right. That was where it all got muddier. Since Nicole, I had taken a girl called Laura home a few times and a girl called Kelly once; I walked them into our house, bumped into my brother, and felt nothing. I went in there with Liv and was on a knife-edge right at the start.

"T," Abe said, "you 'av got to let it go. Wat 'appened wi Zac is in t' past and this Livia girl woz always a short-term prospect. Bev'ly sed that Cheryl sed she'd seen her in the toilets and she got a packet of Dettol wipes out of 'er bag n cleaned the tap before she washed 'er 'ands. Yeah, she's hot, and I can see why you want a bit of posh pussy, but man, don't take this t' wrong way, but she's a freekin' snob. Your far too good for 'er."

My mouth twitched into a smile; I could imagine Livia in the toilet, looking around, hoping nobody was watching her clean that bloody tap.

And Abe was right—I was a good person. I'd done well at college, I worked hard, and I paid my way. I wasn't racist or sexist and, ironically, the only people who I discriminated against were the rich, judgemental, exploitative bastards who came from Livia's world. I gave respect where it was due. I looked after my Mam and Dad. I gave my spare coins to charity. I helped people lift their pushchairs onto the bus. I'd done the shopping for the woman who lived two doors down since her husband died. I smiled a bit more.

"I love her, Abe. She's fucked up but she's the right woman...in the wrong world. That's why I wanted to destroy Zac. But cos I love 'er I'm going to let her go. Get her life back on track."

"Man, the right woman will come, yeah. But it's not somebody who'll build you up an' then drop ya like a shit in a bog."

He went on and on and told me the round of comments made by my friends and family after we'd left the club. My dad said he thought he'd brought me up with values—apparently, Livia was as bad as a city banker. Riley said he thought Zac was the only one stupid enough to be led by his cock. One of the neighbours said I ought to have more respect than to bring somebody dripping with money into the club to rub their noses in the fact they all had nothing. My mum said I'd marry Livia 'over her dead body because she didn't want a daughter-in-law from Surrey who couldn't understand what she sed'. It went on and on. Oh yeah, it turned out the me and Livia debate was like an episode of Question Time.

"What did Zac say?"

Abe laughed, right to his belly. "He said if he woz you he'd be up her like a rat up a drainpipe. He also sed ev'ry body ought to wind their necks in and leave you alone. Oh, and he punched Declan Green for saying you were a treacherous cun—"

I held up my hand to shut him up. I didn't even know why I asked. Zac had got my back.

"Zac's had a busy night—it's bin sum time since he assaulted three blokes of an evening," I said, dryly. "What do you think?"

"I think you're the nearest thing she's gunna get to a bit of bad boy. Rich girls like a bit of rough now an' then. She'll be bored with you in a week or two—it's not like you gonna take 'er to the Maldives. Walk away and say it's bin nice. She'll drop ya anyway and by then you'll have bin disowned, man, totally disowned. There's gunna be enough raised eyebrows and shitty remarks t' next time you walk into that club as it is. If you turn up we 'er again the old school will prob'ly put you in t' stocks. She seems nice enough but we reckon your just infatuated 'cos she is like, in different league, man. She's not right for you."

"You shouldn't be so judgemental, Abe. How would you like it if people thought there was more chance of catching a leprechaun than getting you to work for a day?"

He chuckled. "They'd probably be right. Anyway, I do work—it takes a lotta effort to win the Premier League with Huddersfield F.C. Hmmm."

"It's a fuckin' game."

"It's all a fuckin' game, T, ya should know that by now." He rubbed my hair and threw me the spare controller for his PlayStation. "Come on, beat me once and I'll let you sleep on me sofa."

"I'll beat you then I'm going 'ome."

On one hand, I dared to hope Liv would come back; on the other, I wanted her to walk away without a fight. Because it was for the best—she was a liability—and, on the flip side, I was always gonna bring her down eventually.

Abe shook his head. "You aint goin' if Loki's still there—it'll be like somethin' out of The Hunger Games. You've got it on ya and he'll be seething—what wiv you hitting him for doin' fuck all."

"He has done somethin. He took the piss out of me!"

"He always takes t' piss out of you!" Abe exclaimed, pointing out the stupidity of my comment. "And what was it you were calling him at t' gym last week?"

I laughed, but only a bit—my mood was dire. "Oh, ahh."

Abe was right and I decided I better stay over. I couldn't talk to Livia because I'd back down and not set her free, and I couldn't see Zac or our bones and bits of the house would end up broken. It wasn't long till morning—the sofa would have to do.

Chapter 23

Livia

It was ten-am and I was still in a state of phantasmagoria. Between the images of the live sex show and extreme violence, I could not begin to comprehend the mess in my head. Russ was not the person who I thought. With his reserved ways and thoughtful words, I assumed he was from an educated though not a particularly affluent family, possibly a bit of a loner, and definitely a pacifist. It turned out he was from amongst the roughest people in the area, a fringe member of a gang, and had people reeling in fear due to his aggressive reputation.

I could not see a way.

I could not see a way to bridge the widening gap between us but I could feel it, it was there. He was not just the key to my happiness and my sanity; I genuinely felt he was the only way I could have a worthwhile future.

Five-minutes later, the coffee machine was on and my phone was stuck to my ear as I repeatedly tried to call Russ. I planned to apologise for running out on him but after that I had no idea what to say. I hoped my apology would pave the way for a full explanation of the Nicole situation, tell me Beverly was nothing to him, and inform me he was moving away from the scary estate. Last of all, I hoped he would ask me to be his girlfriend for real.

I was sure I could get over everything if I could deal with the paranoia I felt towards the other girls in his life. On the other hand, I suspected it was all done—it was pie in the sky from the start and the previous night had simply confirmed the harsh reality: a harsh reality that was too much for my sheltered mind to take.

Regardless, nothing was said as he didn't pick up his phone and so I decided to drink my coffee, get dressed, and go to his house to find him.

The Porsche looked out of place and incredibly vulnerable against the backdrop of the grey concrete houses and neglected streets, but not half as vulnerable as I looked when the door opened and I came face-to-face with

Margo, her arms folded across her ample bosom and her face solemn and flushed.

"I am so sorry about last night," I started. Margo gestured for me to go inside. "I don't know how things got so bad. Is Russ out of bed?"

Margo, as polite as she was, offered me a cup of tea I did not want to drink before she began her explanations.

"Things got so bad cos that's who my boys are and you should av never been 'ere."

"But I didn't do anything," I said.

The older woman passed me a mug; I turned it away from the chip before I took a sip.

"You didn't need to. Look love, you may think I'm stupid, but my fam'ly—those boys, are my world. All I care about is keeping 'em safe. There are some things a mother must do—love em, accept em, fight their corner, and say what needs to be sed. And this needs to be sed. With everythin that's 'appened, there's too much 'istory for Russ to turn up 'ere with a girl like you and not be ready to blow. You were always gonna be trouble. I want you to stay away from my lad. As nice as you seem, and as taken as Russell is, you aren't like us and I don't want any more bother dividin' my fam'ly."

I slapped my forehead, frustrated. "Is he in and will somebody please tell me what's going on behind the scenes here?"

"I will." The voice belonged to the brother who I did not want to see. "He's not in. He took off last night. He'll be at Abe's. Come on, I'll walk yer 'round."

I nodded—prepared to go anywhere to just find him. I thanked Margo for the tea and left the house.

"Chuffing hell! Is this yours?" he asked, eyes agog on seeing my car.

"Yes. Get in and direct me to Abe's house please."

Zac offered a lopsided grin before sliding onto the elevated passenger seat.

"It's actually his Mam's house and ya need to take the left at the end of this road."

I was very divided. In spite of the undercurrent of unrest and the events of the previous night, I liked Zac—I was drawn to him almost. He was incredibly personable, smiley, and warm—in spite of his smashed-up face and antagonistic tendencies.

"Will Beverly have stopped there too?"

"Fraid so, love. Doubt he'll av shagged her though."

"How comforting," I returned dryly. "Now, you said you'd tell me about all of this cloak and dagger stuff. I assume it's something to do with this Nicole girl he refuses to talk about."

"Hmmm. Next road on your right and flipping heck, we thought she was upper class cos her folks bought her a Rav 4. Who bought you this little beauty?"

"I bought it myself," I returned curtly; "now tell me the freeking story before I hit you myself."

"Kinky. Though you better not tell our kid you asked me to play slap and tickle." Zac chuckled. "I'll keep it short n sweet. He hasn't told you because he's still raw as fuck. My bro was with this girl, Nicole, for years before he brought her 'ome. After he did, things started goin' tits up. She knew her rich parents would rather cut off their hands than give their blessing for her to be with him an' the arguing started. Anyway, they split up and he moved out and went to stop wiv some mates. A few weeks later, she phoned me and asked me to go 'round for the rest of 'is stuff cos she didn't want to see him. I went 'round and she tells me how he'd dumped 'er because he didn't love her any more, cries, and gives me all the shit. I ended up in bed with her."

"You fucking arse."

"I thought they were finished. I'd av never done it if I thought they were together and I didn't know he loved her at the time. I thought she was a bit of a rich plaything. She was a bit thick to be honest—not his type."

"But the bed was still bloody warm."

Zac raised an eyebrow of disapproval and I realised, yet again, why so many women fell into his bed—there was something about him.

"Stop here. Behind that van. Anyway, the story gets worse. Me and her swore each other to secrecy. A month later, he turned up at home in a right fuckin' mess. He tells us they're back together cos she's pregnant and he doesn't want his kid living in a single parent home. He couldn't work out how it happened—they always used jonnies—but she made up a load of crap and said one must av split. A few weeks later the fickle cow decides she's getting rid of the baby and he spent ages trying to persuade her to keep it. He woz gutted cos she was killin' his kid. He cried. He actually fucking cried in front of me. I felt like hanging myself with guilt. Then on the day after t' abortion, Russ went fucking mental and she admitted it was mine. He dumped her, came home, and had a go at killing me in front of half the estate. And yeah, I deserved it, before ya say it."

"Oh my god." I assumed they had just fallen out over the girl—I had no inclination that his brother had gotten her pregnant and Russ went through the trauma of somebody aborting a baby he thought was his. "But he said she'd dumped him."

"No, he left 'er. She wanted 'im back. She still does—texts him and sends the odd letter begging for forgiveness. He's a good lad, me bro, and she realises how fuckin' stupid she's bin. I've only told you all this cos I don't want you to think he's a psycho. He's probably not told you to protect my shittin' ass. Do ya want me to come in with you?"

I nodded. Zac followed me out the car and then knocked on the door.

"Morning Bev, is our Russ 'ere?" Zac asked.

I stood coyly at his side with an overwhelming urge to ask the girl if she had laid a finger on my boyfriend.

"Yeah Zac, are you comin' in or shall I send 'im out?"

Zac turned and sauntered off. "We'll wait in t' car."

Russ did not look happy when he reached the vehicle; he glared at his brother and was very stand-offish with me. I dropped Zac home and we made the journey to my abode in painful silence.

Chapter 24

Livia

It was strange walking through the front door and into the grand foyer with Russ; he usually used my French doors as he was invariably muddy and he didn't want to draw the attention of the rest of the people who lived there. He kicked off his shoes and plodded to one of the stools at my kitchen island. I switched on the kettle.

I wanted him to tell me he had not slept with Beverly; I wanted to apologise profusely for my rash behaviour the night before; I wanted to hug him but there seemed to be a tall, impermeable barrier between us.

"Babe, I'm sorry for walking out on you last night," I uttered, ashamed. "Did you sleep with the girl?"

"Bev'ly? No, I slept on the sofa." He looked up from his hands. "I can't believe you call me babe."

Neither could I. Jealous, possessive, clingy and calling him babe. I had actually lost my mind.

"And I'm sorry you saw me kick off like a belligerent. And saw that lassie sucking Loki's cock. He 'as this impediment—runs on instinct rather than sense. He always 'as. It's no wonder he's always in shit," he told me.

"I can't believe how judgemental I am," I admitted. "I hated it there, Russ. I don't want you to live amongst that coarseness and violence. Why don't you come to live with me?"

I said it. I meant it. I couldn't believe it.

Russ shook his head. "I can't. I can't pay my way here and I don't want charity. They're all right, Liv. I was wrong. This is never goin' to work. It never was. I'm gonna cut my ties and walk away so you can get the right man for your life."

"No! What? And who's right?"

The tiny fibres in my wool sweater prickled my skin; I pulled it away from my neck, feeling strangled.

"Everybody, Livia. Your friends. My friends. My family—your family if you asked em. My feckin' deep-down-inside sensible voice. What do your friends think about me and you?"

I felt my cheeks redden. "They think I'm living out a fantasy before I settle down and tie the knot with Kieran. They don't think we could work. They don't think I've got it in me to let my family down and go home with anybody other than an affluent, successful guy."

He nodded. "Yeah, my friends think the same. Reckon you're just playing me cos I'm the safest, nearest thing you're gonna get to a bit of bad boy. They reckon you'll get bored when I can't take you anywhere nice. They reckon I'm infatuated cos you're out of my league. They think I'd get sick of bein' made to feel inferior. They also reckon I'm a traitor and I've sold out on my morals for, I quote, 'a bit of posh pussy'."

And on that, I started to cry.

"Liv, I'm a realist. Your family and friends don't want you marryin' me—they want you marrying the suave businessman you were paying for sex. Not that you needed to pay. He was only tiptoeing around cos he thought it's what you wanted."

I shook my head to dislodge the harsh words. "No, Russ. No."

"Liv, for somebody so smart you can be really thick. Can you picture my family and mates in a wedding marquee in Surrey? My Mam in her chain store dress—knocking back pints and needing a Derbyshire slang to Queen's English translator. My Dad ranting—punching the air for the working classes—scorning at anyone who didn't do manual labour. My brother wouldn't even be in the tent—he'd be around the back shagging every girl over the age of consent. As if your family would accept me when I came with that! And I wouldn't want my folks to alter. I love them for who they are. It was great while it lasted but you need to get back on track before you destroy your life and me in the process."

"I couldn't give a shit what my family think," I replied.

"You would. And you give a shit about your work and you know I won't fit in there. What happens when we're at the black-tie event and the drunk guy comes pawing over you? Kieran wud say, 'now now chap, I think you've had a little too much champagne'. I'd just break his nose and you'd probably get sacked."

It was true. Cruelly true.

"But I love you, Russ."

"And I love you. I really do. With your OCDs and your inability to empty your dishwasher…"

I glanced up and he smiled at me. He was telling the truth and, for a moment, I thought we would make it.

"But love, Liv… I doubt it'll be enough to cross the social boundary between us. You'll never be able to abandon the polish that wealth puts on your existence. I'll never abandon my spade and become one of the half-corpses the corporation gives a computer and pays to perform. I'm not a performing chimp just like you're not a lower-class drone. Love is making sacrifices—it's not always clear what they'll be at the start."

I reached for his hands, his calloused weathered hands, and pulled them towards me. "Let's pretend the rest of the world doesn't happen. Please."

"We can for a week. For a month. For a year, maybe. But it'll get us in the end and this will feel even worse. Shame will divide us. You were ashamed of me when you saw where I lived—how I fought with my brother. I was ashamed of you judged those people with their broken teeth."

"We judge because we are afraid. I'm just afraid."

I looked long and hard at his hat-bed-hat wayward hair and the stubble that had never been designer.

"Yeah, me too. I'm scared of you ruining your life because of me. Shunned by your family. Cast out by your friends. Out on a limb at work. You need the high-flying business man. The ten-bedroom country home. The flash holidays. The two kids with their private education. You deserve it, Livia. You're a good person underneath those designer clothes. I was always the lowly groundkeeper in your little fantasy. Just leave it there, yeah."

And then it all became apparent. In years gone by I had liked the Michelin starred restaurants, the dinner parties, wine bars, luxurious holidays, and nice cars. Perhaps I would get bored with the chip shop. Perhaps I would be embarrassed when he turned up at my work in trainers and then said fuck. Perhaps I would start to feel awkward about paying for the holidays when he clearly felt like he was my charity case. He would still enjoy going to his 'Mam's' on a Sunday for lunch, whereas I would want to take a meat thermometer as I knew the oven thermostat was broken. Russ was insightful and principled and if he was prepared to cut off his nose to spite his face then it must be the right thing to do. I probably would resent him eventually and he would resent me, and then we would destroy each other after we had broken the ties with our friends, families, and worlds.

Perhaps he was right. Perhaps love was not enough.

Russ drained the contents of his cup, placed a chaste kiss on my lips, and drew me close. And then he was gone.

The bath was hot and bubbly but it did nothing to soak away my misery. I cried, profaned, and cried some more, and then I decided to do something assertive. Our story had gone well off track; I'd had a taste of the happily ever after and I could no longer settle for anything less.

In an abhorrent waste of approximately one-hundred and twenty litres of hot water, I got straight out of the bath, threw on some gym pants and a top, and wrote a quick letter. I did not have time to dally; I was due to represent the company at a charity ball that evening and I needed to go to Russ' house and persuade him to give us another chance first.

To my disappointment, Adam, not Russ, opened the door.

"Hi, Adam. Is Russ in?"

"Nope. Not seen 'im since last night. Zac said he was at your 'ouse."

Shit. I was kind of stuck; I could not wait around and so I gave Adam the letter and asked him to give it to Russ when he got home. I left as quickly as I had arrived, booted the car all the way home, and exchanged the long bath for a quick shower. I had a little black dress to get into.

Chapter 25

Russ

As suburbia re-appeared, the houses became closer together and the colour drained from the world. I felt dismal. My shoes were full of concrete and my mind a shit-storm fuelled by every last bit of energy I could muster.

Deep down, I hoped Livia would tell me that where I was going was more important than from where I came. I'd hoped she would fight for us and tell me the big house and the flashy lifestyle weren't so important to her. But she didn't: she accepted what I said and cried. And that confirmed what I knew. I'd tried my hardest—so fucking hard. I'd come from a place where my most valued skill was having the bollocks to stand and fight. I'd been 'educated' in a school from which leaving with a fistful of GCSEs took divine intervention. But I'd come good—yeah, I'd come good. Kept my nose clean, got a job, and made a good start on a solid future. I'd dared to hope that perhaps being honest and genuine would be enough—but it wasn't.

Livia wasn't strong enough to stand up to the disapproval and I wasn't worthy of the trade with the rich bloke who could buy her the world. I was worried about her, of course I was, but I knew she'd be alright; she knew she could address her issues one at a time and I knew Kieran would be in the wings to save the day in his gold-plated chariot.

And I was shredded inside. In fucking tatters. It was much worse than before—a million times worse than when I'd thought I had lost my child and brother, and I had lost the girl I loved. But to love was to sacrifice. To love was to give and I had decided I would give whatever it took. I'd have dealt with my family and stood up to my friends. I'd have put up with the judgment and the disapproval. But Livia wouldn't. Or couldn't. I could not be sure.

By the time I made it home, I felt like I could disappear into a pile of regret or resentment—that was if the blisters on my feet didn't kill me first. I soon met the piercing stare of my father who, for once, held back his lectures and prophecies and handed me a folded-up bit of paper. My stomach lurched.

Russ,

I want to be with you. I want to be with you so

much. My friends and family will think I am crazy

but I don't care. I can take their rejection; I just

can't take yours.

I want to share your world. I need you to share my sky.

We can get the happily ever after.

Love you, babe x

The girl was prepared to fight; perhaps she was strong enough to take on the shit after all. And it was all it took. I put the note in my pocket and was out of the front door and on my bike without a thought.

I had no idea what I was going to say when I got to her house.

Intuition.

I was going on that.

Chapter 26

Livia

I stepped out of the shower cubicle and wrapped a towel around my body. The towel hit the polished floor when I curled my hands around the vanity unit and stared at the woman looking back at me in the mirror. For many years, my life had taken place in a privileged bubble; I was isolated from hardship and inequality inside my blissful enclosure. And then, because of Russ, I realised that the outside world was harsh and insentient and I felt utterly blank. I looked utterly blank too: a blank canvas awaiting its covering.

Within the next hour the wet, dark hair draggling around my chin would be blow-dried and glossy, and teased into its expensively trimmed style and finished using sprays and serums. My bare skin would be covered with Elemis and Clinique as I pampered my skin and enhanced my features. By the time I put on my knee-length, black dress my deceptive illusion would be complete. Jesus, I was questioning everything and I was not sure I could play my part for much longer.

A knock at the door broke my wayward contemplation and my heart flipped on the assumption that Russ had got the letter and come back. I snatched the towel from the floor, wrapped it around my chest, and was tucking it in when I opened the door leading to the foyer.

"Kieran!" I exclaimed, my disappointment apparent.

Black tuxedo. Polished shoes. *Oh, shit.*

"Come in." I shuffled away from the door—terribly self-conscious due to my lack of attire. "I texted you to say I was driving. I drank too much last night and I don't want to stay late."

"Livia," he said dismissively, "the car was already booked. We can play it by ear with the return journey. I'm easy; I'm only going tonight to build bridges."

"Okay." Although I was unhappy going to the event with him, it was logical now he was there. "I'll just get ready. I'm running a bit late."

I slipped my lipstick into my clutch bag and arrived in the lounge as a hairy face appeared at the glass door. My elation was brief and had totally vacated by the time Russ walked in and acknowledged the suited man sitting on my sofa.

And then I said the worse thing possible. "This is not how it looks."

"How is that, Liv?" Russ' words were bitter; his face etched with hurt and disappointment. "Like you were so embarrassed of me you said tonight's invite was for one so you could take James Bond instead?"

Kieran did look like a ready-to-roll James Bond. Russ, on the other hand, looked homeless. He wore jeans crumpled from a night on his friend's sofa and there was blood on his shirt; his face was distended from fighting and ruddy from exertion. But I wanted him; I wanted him for his yet-to-be-cleaned teeth and his chain store clothes.

I shook my head though I knew my reddened cheeks made me look guilty as charged. "No. I was going alone. Kieran just turned up. Well. Tell Russ I'm telling the truth, Kieran!"

"It's true," Kieran offered reluctantly.

"Kieran, please go to the car and give us some space."

Russ about turned and headed back to the door. "Don't bother. Him being here now 'as said everything. I believed your bullshit, Livia—but it turns out everybody else was right."

I got to the door in time to see him pull the bike from the gravelled forecourt, sling a leg over the frame, and pedal away into the dark. He was gone and his interpretation of the scene had made everything definite to him. Russ knew Kieran was the 'pretend boyfriend' I took everywhere and he wasn't to know the invite was singular and that Kieran was personally invited through his business. I knew Russ thought I was ashamed of him and, although not ashamed, I had been very reluctant to take him to events that were pivotal to my career. But those thoughts were firmly in the past; I no longer cared what people thought—they could take me with him or not at all.

"Sorry," Kieran muttered, as I stared into the darkness. "You could phone him and attempt to force an explanation or you could be sensible, accept the fling for what it was, and move on."

"If I want your opinion regarding my relationship, I'll ask for it. And there is no point in phoning—he won't pick up." I grabbed a Kleenex and dabbed under my eyes. "I've fucked up. I've really fucked up. Let's just go."

I began with a little Filo pastry tart filled with mozzarella cheese and sundried tomato. It was a difficult choice; I initially veered to the roasted yellow peppers, stuffed with cream cheese, but the pastry cups were golden and delightfully crunchy. Having devoured the tart, I caught the attention of a waitress carrying a platter loaded with sliced cucumber, piled high with fresh salmon and snipped chives. I always assumed the *hors d'oeuvres* served as foreplay, a colourful teaser imparting an indication of what would arrive for the main meal, but how I was wrong. I could have circulated around those silver trays and ate my way through the entire evening and, considering the clients I had come to secure were conspicuous by their absence, I briefly considered it. And I would have if it wasn't for the distraction—the reason for the event—an exhibition and auction organised by a corporately-funded charity which aimed to encourage unprivileged, talented young people into art.

I was transfixed, absolutely transfixed, by a small piece painted by the young woman who was nervously chewing her nails nearby. In all honesty, it wasn't the most impressive thing I'd ever seen but it called to me. Off-centre was a galaxy-like swirl of colour, all red and orange, sharp and shallow—the lines were defined but with little intensity. Around the outside of the canvas were soft, blended purple-blue finger-like projections. The reds were surrounded and held by the blue, forming regions of deep velvety purple—delving, encompassing regions of chromatic warmth. Every meeting point between the opposing sides was different and novel and drew my eye.

"Do ya like it?" a frail voice asked.

I turned to see the artist, who was about nineteen, with a red, asymmetrical haircut. She wore cheap black trousers, shiny due to the polyester content, and a white cotton t-shirt adorned with black floral prints. My heart extended out to her. I saw a girl who had trawled her wardrobe for her best clothes and still felt awkward beside the exhibitions of wealth around her. I grinned and then remembered the sadness associated with my emotional connection.

"I love it. It feels like me and somebody who I love and have lost. That was me before." I pointed at the frantic centre. "And that is him." I moved my finger to the periphery. "He is calm and rich and has perspective. The meeting of the colour is us. Soothing my upset, giving me depth where before there was superficial nothingness."

The girl studied my face; she saw the rich woman with her three-hundred-pound handbag, and wondered if a person without a life of suffering could ever experience emotional depth. She looked at me pitifully; I was not expecting her pity and it sent me terribly off kilter. I knew of the girl—what with my company heavily backing the project. She had spent eight-years in foster care and was a controversial beneficiary, having qualified for the charity grant after a conviction for shoplifting following the theft of a can of deodorant and a pack of chicken breasts.

And I realised, I absolutely realised, that I no longer judged the girl for pinching that chicken: I judged the social stratification that allowed half of society to scrape good food into the bin while there were so many who stole it out of desperation.

We stared until the interaction became painful and then, in her thick dialect, she said: "Bin in the shallows and then goin' out deep teks bravery. An' if you were a flat surface n' he gave you depth, it wasn't a waste a time."

She had said it all.

I had been lost in the shallows: the crystal clear, topaz waters, where crazily, I couldn't even breathe. I never wanted to go there again; I wanted the depths—as complex and dark and uncertain as they could be. I wanted to be lulled by the waves of love and not those of possession.

The girl peered over my shoulder, at the man who had heard my every word. He held out his hand and silently implored with me to take it.

I turned to the girl. "How much is this piece expected to fetch at the auction?"

She shrugged. "A few hundred quid."

"I'll give you five-thousand pounds if you pull it from the sale."

At my exuberant suggestion, her Kohl-lined eyes nearly popped out of her head. The proceeds for the tickets and donations went to the foundation but only thirty-percent of the sales revenue—the rest went to the artist and that would provide her with an unimaginable amount of money.

"God yeah," she stammered. "Are you serious?"

"Absolutely."

I turned to the man standing patiently behind me. I interpreted his expression; there were things to be said.

We walked silently towards the foyer and stopped in an alcove where, to my surprise, he kissed me. His lips were firm and functional, and he tasted of Listerine—not of fresh air and Colgate and happiness.

"You don't need to buy the picture, Livia. You can have the dream. We can become deep and strong. Let's make something permanent."

I was blindsided. "Are you in love with me?"

"I care about you. A lot. I've done head-over-heels crazy before and it doesn't work. Not for long. We could be good together. You know we could." I gazed on, wordless. "Livia?"

"What are you doing here?" I returned, confused.

"Trying to win you. Please abandon the fling. This guy. He's not right for you. He's rough. Coarse. He has nothing to offer, whereas I can give you the world."

Kieran's face was perfect. Square jaw. Straight nose. Perfect smile. But his eyes were flat. No warmth. No hint of mischief. Or contemplation. Or unpredictability.

"Do you know how to make a fire?" I asked, my head tipped to the side.

"Why the hell would I need to make a fire?"

"Because fire is what draws a person out of the shadows. It's the heat to our cold. It's the light in the dark."

He scoffed. "Livia. I have central heating. A heater in my car. Electricity in my house. I don't need a fucking fire."

"And that, Kieran, is where you are so very, very wrong."

I didn't care that Kieran was looking down on me; with his superiority and the props which made him. Because Russ had taught me how to make fire. Not that I needed to—because Russ had enough fire for the pair of us.

I just needed to get him back.

Chapter 27

Russ

Every eye was on us as we walked up the stairs at the nightclub. Beverly was wearing a pair of tiny grey shorts which left nothing to the imagination. And yeah, she had the body of a lingerie model. Long legs. A flat stomach. An arse most women would kill for. Her black, curly hair was untied and there was something shiny on her perfect lips. She was by far the most stunning girl there and I knew people were wondering how the hell I'd managed to get somebody like her on my arm. That was easy; it was because the woman I wanted had dumped me for a slicker, richer bloke and I was pissed off and kicking out like a teenager. Within the next hour I'd kiss Beverly and, before the night was over, I'd probably sleep with her knowing full well it would make me feel shit. But feeling shit happened. Feeling shit happened a lot. I expected no other. At the top of the pecking order, a person expected everything to be good; at the bottom, we expected most things to be rubbish. I only hoped the good times would outweigh the bad in the end.

I hadn't been clubbing for years but as soon as I felt the music it was back in me. Surreal lighting. Synthetic drums that shake your insides—they always took me to a different place and, god, I needed to be there. I was disillusioned and angry.

Beverly took my hand and towed me to the bar where she shouted into my ear and asked me what I wanted to drink. I scanned the rows of brightly coloured bottles and shrugged. I didn't care. I just wanted to get pissed.

A few minutes later, an ice-cold alcopop was shoved in my hand and, after a grimace, I drank the lot. I went back to the bar and Beverly found a space to dance. I watched her. She was beautiful and free. Beverly was not tied by social expectation and, because of it, she was liberated. I wanted Livia to get her liberation—it would have been a privilege to be a part of it but it was not meant to be and I was bitter—really fucking bitter.

We drank another two bottles of pungent alcohol while we stood, close together, shouting over the music. And then we abandoned the words and headed to the gathering of bodies. A track in and Beverly smiled broadly, her pearly whites glowing under the UV lights. She threw her arms around my neck.

"We ought to av dropped some Es, Russell."

I shook my head. "Nah. Not done an E in years."

And then she kissed me and her lemon tainted tongue touched mine. I kissed her back but it did nothing for me. Not like kissing Liv, when even the touch of her lips made my self-control do one. Beverly's leg pressed between mine and she ground onto my thigh. I knew her game.

I pulled my mouth from hers. "You're still a dirty cow then, Bev'ly!"

Beverly giggled, turned around, and lined her ass up with my crotch as we danced. As the tempo changed, she held up a hand and got the attention of a group of girls and lads who had just appeared at the raised entrance to the dance-floor. Students. They meandered over and, with an arm around my waist, she made shouted introductions. And then I was hit by the wrongness of everything.

"Bev'ly," I yelled in her ear. "Will you be alright if I go? I feel a bit off it."

She stuck out her lip, faking disappointment, but I held firm and said I wanted to leave. Beverly shrugged, grabbed my cheeks, and kissed me.

"I s'pose. Don't be a stranger, yeah!"

I smiled and held up my hand and got out of there as fast as my legs would go. I needed to go home. Mam and Dad were out but my bro was in and I wanted to sit on the sofa and talk rubbish. The bitter retribution had been bad enough; I didn't want the aftereffects of shagging my friend.

I wove down the reveller-strewn streets and pulled out my phone. *Shit.* There were loads of missed calls, including six from Livia. I hadn't heard the phone in the club and I'd forgot to put the bloody thing onto vibrate. My walk broke into a run and I half sped, half stumbled my way to the bus stop.

Livia

Rejecting Kieran was a tremendously heart-wrenching thing to do. I cared for him, I cared for him a lot, but the security, nice times, and the substantial pooled assets would never bring love. And I wanted love; I needed love; I needed the man who I shared it with.

I banged at Russ' door though, to my disappointment, it was not answered by Russ but instead by his brother. I was hit by a wall of warm air and the heavenly smell of homemade treacle sponge and custard. Yet again, Zac was in a state of partial undress; however, unlike the last time, his torso was covered and he was barefoot and wearing shorts. I politely averted my eyes from his legs as he blatantly looked at me from my heels to my hair.

"Hi. Is Russ in?"

"Nope."

I sighed despondently. "Brilliant. I came all this way and he's bloody out."

"Well, you should have phoned him first."

"I did," I returned sharply; "he won't answer his phone."

"You ought to have thought of that before you dumped him an' rubbed his nose in it by shagging the rich guy two minutes later."

"Erm, it was Russ who dumped me and I did not shag anybody. Kieran turned up at my house uninvited and of his own accord," I returned, my voice thick with irritation; "and if your brother had stuck around to hear me out I would have told him just that."

"Come in and I'll phone around to see where he is. He'll probably be at his missus' house."

"His missus?" My bottom lip quivered. "He said…"

Zac laughed, sauntered into the kitchen, and came out carrying a small glass tumbler. "God, Livia, you're well soft. I mean Abe—that big-haired girl he hangs around with. Sit down. I'll give him a call."

I perched on the edge of the sofa and Zac poured a good few inches from the bottle of cheap whiskey which was sitting on the coffee table. He handed it to me before picking up his glass, dialling his brother's number, and getting the same zero response as I had.

"Arse, you must av right pissed him off if he's ignorin' me," he returned, scratching his head. "I'll try Abe." He dialled another number and the call connected after a painfully long amount of time. "All right, Abraham. It's only me, man. 'Av you got our kid wiv you?"

There was a brief pause as the other man returned a comment.

"Clubbing!" Zac exclaimed. "Alan Tichmarsh has gone clubbing—who the bloody hell with?" There was another pause: one which momentarily knocked the wind out of the loquacious man's sails. "Can you try to phone him? And 'er as well. If you get through, tell him his posh bird's here and if he doesn't hurry up and get back home, I'm gonna shag her. That should rush him a bit. Oh, wait, no—don't tell him that—I quite like bin able-bodied and I'm startin' me new job on Monday. Cheers, man."

My heart felt as heavy as a stone. "He's out with Beverly?" Zac nodded. "I cannot believe the day we fall out he goes straight out with her."

Zac tapped my leg. "It's the laws of Newton, Livia. Cause and effect, action and reaction. If you hit somebody on the knee with a little metal hammer, you've got to expect the leg to come kicking back out. Don't worry—he dunt love her—he'll be back in a bit."

"Firstly," I huffed, "are you lot in competition for the philosopher's stone in this house?"

"Nope—my Mam's as thick as shit."

"Secondly, how do you know he doesn't love her?"

"Because he never threatened to kill me if I touched her—I aint shagged her but I flirt like fuck and one time I snogged her in front of him and he never batted an eyelid."

"How can you be so casual about intimacy?"

"Sex isn't intimate. The most intimate stuff a person 'as is what's in here." He tapped his head. "It's the only thing that can be given but not taken."

"And as for shagging me—whatever makes you think I would lay a finger on you?"

He laughed. "Oh come on, Livia, if you weren't with my little bro we'd be at it like rabbits by now. I charmed the knickers off a real-life nun once."

"Did you now. Do you actually think about anything other than sex?"

Zac nodded and grinned. "Yeah. Family, mates, having a good time, and hey, I start a plumbing apprenticeship next week—get me."

I downed my drink and he poured me another.

"That's if I can make it in. Our kid might have put me in hospital by then," he said, chuckling.

"I can't believe you are so insouciant over something so serious. At what point is the two of you beating each other funny?"

"It's not, but it's one of those things."

I glared at him. "Why are you so horrible to him? Why do you wind him up?"

"Cos I do. Just like he winds me up. He gives as good as he gets—you just aint seen it. Livia, drink up and stop bickering with me."

Driven by alcohol, my mouth opened before my brain engaged. "God, there is something about you that really pisses me off."

"I know. You piss me off. And do you know why—it's because if you climbed out your arse and dropped your rar-rah social pleasantries, you'd realise me and you are more alike than you think."

My eyes roamed the length of his hairy legs, and rested on his bruised, swollen face. "Oh yes," I said, with a look of disbelief; "I can see the resemblance."

"Not how we look, you goon—it's called allure— sex appeal."

"You are quite honestly the most arrogant, big-headed man I have ever met. What makes you so certain you are irresistible?"

"Nobody 'as ever sed no so I must be! Women like 'ow I look and most importantly, I make em feel special and make em laugh."

I shook my head. "I doubt you could do anything to make me laugh right now."

Grinning, he looked right at me. "Is that a bet?"

I held out my hand and he shook it. "It certainly is."

Zac stood up, tapped his lip and narrowed his eyes. "Right, given the circumstances and that miserable face of yours, I'll av to go in hard."

"Is that right…"

Zac grabbed my ankles and pulled until only my back was on the sofa. Amidst my squeals, he knelt between my legs, yanked the hem of my dress up to my ribs, and revealed my stocking tops, a scrap of lace which constituted as knickers, and my stomach. Following which, and to my utmost shock, he blew a big, wet raspberry on my skin. And I laughed. I laughed because I was stunned—astounded as to the extent of his inappropriate actions—and because it was very ticklish. As the next flesh-slapping raspberry landed, I tried to push his head away; it was some time since my last toilet trip and the giggling and pressure on my abdomen was making me dangerously close to wetting myself.

"Zac, stop it," I said seriously. "No, Zac. No. Stop. Please. Stop."

The door flew open.

"Get off 'er. Get off 'er you pig," Margo yelled.

And then all hell broke loose.

Russ barged in and saw Zac kneeling between my legs, his face in line with my underwear and the dress hitched above my waist. He vaulted the sofa and threw his brother into the 1980's gas fire before I could voice my protest.

The silver grid clattered onto the tiled hearth and the white ceramic back-plates shattered and fell. Russ yelled and swore and, when Zac found his feet, kicked him in the face and sent him crashing into the brass ornaments scattered on the hearth. Russ was in front of Zac, his eyes wild and his fists flailing, taking blow upon blow from Zac's thrashing feet.

I shouted for them to stop, I screamed and pleaded, but my words were lost amongst Margo's screams followed by the sound of Zac crashing, back-first, through the glass coffee table. He held up his hands and tried the voice of reason before, I supposed, the instinct for survival kicked in and he retaliated.

It was horrible.

Absolutely horrible.

And there was so much blood. Russ' nose had exploded and was leaking down his face: the face marred with the blood from Zac's bleeding fists. I was so scared—so very scared. They were both hurt, bleeding and swaying and fighting for breath, but still they fought on.

It took Adam and two of the neighbours to separate Russ and Zac. Russ was bleeding heavily though was not as injured as his brother. Zac was in a bad way—he'd been thrown through a table and repeatedly kicked and punched in the face and body. Barely clinging onto consciousness, his head lolled; he clutched his abdomen, and he drew pained, shallow breaths.

I reached Russ as the neighbours released his arms.

"Oh no. What have you done?" I pulled Russ close. "What have you done."

Due to the shouting and crashing and extreme violence, nobody saw Margo leave the room to call nine-nine-nine. The ambulance arrived shortly before the police and I watched, distraught and devastated, as Zac was taken away on a spinal board and Russ was bundled into the back of a police car, his hands cuffed behind his back

Epilogue

Livia

It had been a particularly dull, taxing day and I was glad to be home and setting my tired eyes on my ruffled husband and our two (rather large) boys. Daniel arrived when Russ was twenty-six and Thomas arrived when he was twenty-seven. It transpired that, not only was the morning after pill less than one-hundred percent effective, but we were the most fertile couple in Britain and I was abnormally resistant to hormonal contraceptives.

Russ held out an arm, I settled between his legs, and his calming soul replaced my anxiety with peace. I averted my eyes to the granite surface of the island. Durex. And the reason for the furtive faces of our sons became clear.

"Right lads. Rule number one. Get it bagged. If you pole up and tell us you've got some lassie up the duff, you're out on your arse."

I smiled. I couldn't help it—he still didn't have it in him to call a spade a fork.

"Dad, I'm not stupid," Daniel stammered.

"Son, I'm not stupid, but still, you're here because me and ya mother had an 'accident' in a restaurant toilet," he flatly told him.

I glowed and ran my nose down the four-days-worth of beard on Russ' cheek.

"Not in our bed. Not if we're in the house," Russ said, most seriously. "Or you'll have me to deal with."

Both boys nodded; they did not cross their father.

"Have you done, babe?"

"Yep."

I got off his knee. "You have a lovely party, boys," I said, pulling their protesting frames into a hug.

Russ smiled at me and winked, and I went to change for our date night: fish and chips and a few hours of romance in the two-man tent on the lawn.

It was the same tent. The same bodged together sleeping bag. Russ wouldn't buy new until the old was beyond repair.

Sixteen years earlier, I had told my parents I was carrying a child belonging to a man who was on the national minimum wage and who had a conviction for ABH—in spite of Zac's refusal to testify. They were gutted. They said we would never last. They said I should not settle for a man lacking prospects—who could not provide me with the life I deserved. The talk of Russ being unable to provide, however, stopped soon after he became a father.

Because provision is not synonymous with wealth.

Russ could give us food, water, and keep us dry and warm. He helped with the night feeds and did bath time; he changed nappies and cleaned up the vomit; he taught our children to swim and ride a bike; he was there at parent's evening and helped with the homework; he established the boundaries and taught them the meaning of the word no; and then he got up in the morning, did a day of manual labour and, a lot of the time, came home and made the dinner. The boys and I always came first, the office or the promotion never got a mention, and several people around me ate a very large slice of envy-laced humble pie.

I had support.

I had immeasurable love.

I had everything.

Including a wonderful extended family who were spiritually rich and admirably outspoken. Not bland or infected with the destructive disease which is consumerism. The family who taught me that the less people own, the more they share. They were gelled together by a lack of possession whereas my affluent family were segregated by an excess of it: six bedrooms, four reception rooms, five televisions, four computers—we were like honey-bloated, solitary bees in a communal hive: spoiled and isolated—conditions that Russ would never allow in our home. We shared a table every night. Come rain or shine, we walked together on a Sunday afternoon. We handed down clothes. The boys shared a game's console. Lunch was regularly leftovers from the night before. Our hardworking, well-mannered boys were not spoiled. Not by money anyway.

We proved that the only currency which really matters is not counted in pounds: it is measured in amounts—kindness, goodness, and morality. It turns out that money is not an obstacle, but instead a drug with the power to poison or starve. It is also an excuse for bad behaviour and prejudice, as is the invention that is class: the reversible division of society by the unfair distribution of wealth, false ideals, and poor education.

Russ and I crossed the two-way street of discrimination and we found something special. Perfect. The reason we were made; him on a council estate in the Midlands and me in a picture-perfect village in Surrey. In many ways, we are different—but difference is good. Russ says that difference makes us strong: it is the indifference which could pull us apart. And he is right. We are strong. Stronger than any couple I know. Seventeen years on.

Author's note

Three years ago, I decided to turn from science and learn to write. However, as a working mother who could not spell, plot, or punctuate, the straight-forward premise and the gruelling reality turned out to be very different things. So, please bear with me...I am trying—I really am!

Anyway, whilst I continue to bang my head against the wall with my later stuff, I've decided to inflict Share My Sky on the world in an attempt to do something, anything, to take a step towards my dream job in writing and the escape from the evil clutches of a mortgage.

And so, thank you for taking time to read my contemporary fairy tale and I hope it made you smile. If you enjoyed Share My Sky, I would be so very grateful if you could find the time to leave a rating/review on Amazon. Reviews are so very important to independent authors and could be the difference between me succeeding or crying into my wine on a nightly basis.

Wish me luck!

Printed in Great Britain
by Amazon